NIYAH ZURI
AND
THE PHARAOH'S
THRONE

NIYAH ZURI
AND
THE PHARAOH'S
THRONE

Anna Nyakana

Second Edition

First Edition published December 2016

ISBN 978-1-7350911-1-2

Niyah Zuri Books

P.O. Box 270418

West Hartford, CT 06127

www.annanyakana.com

Additional literary works by Anna Nyakana

Niyah Zuri and The Mayan Eclipse

The Student Survival Guide to Online College

For

Judah Mukubwa

Conquering Lion of the Tribe of Judah
Hailing from the Klan of Mukubwa

and

Osiris Omugabe

God of Resurrection, King of Ankole, Giver of Freedom

CONTENTS

PART I
POWER OF THREE

PART II
ASCENDING THE THRONE

PART 1

POWER OF THREE

1

REACHING LOTUS

The heavy clouds burst with rain the day the Zuri family moved into their new home. Niyah stared out of the car window as rain drops pounded against the glass, wondering if she would ever make new friends at her new school. Blowing a curl of hair out of her face, she remembered the adventures at her old apartment in the busy city and wondered what sort of things she would discover in the *boring* suburbs.

"Probably just air...clean air...and trees...lots of trees," Niyah thought.

She dug deep into her front pocket, retrieving her loyal compass, and watched the red needle as it spun in circles; anytime Niyah felt lost her compass would always lead the way. The compass was a birthday gift from her father when she turned nine and it traveled across the vast <u>Atlantic Ocean</u> from <u>Tanzania</u> in East Africa. Niyah's *favorite* feature about her compass was the bearing, the part of the compass that held everything together in the center. The bearing was bejeweled with a rare orange sapphire called <u>Padparadscha</u>; the gem radiated in the sunlight and glowed beautifully in the darkness. Wrinkling her brow, Niyah studied the final direction of the needle pointing west and with a sigh put it away in her pocket. She gazed out of the car window once again, counting the trees as they drove further away from downtown.

"I could build a treehouse at least...maybe add a zip-line extension to the house," Niyah pondered, beginning to sketch a blueprint in her mind of the design.

"Niyah," called Mr. Zuri, as he looked in the rear-view mirror, "I can see the worry on your face sweetheart. Number one: *Relax*, you will make plenty of new friends and number two: you'll finally have your own room!"

"I know, thanks Dad," said Niyah, managing a slight smile.

"This is going to be a *good* change for our family!" said Mrs. Zuri to both Niyah and her twelve-year-old brother

Isaiah, who seemed to be distracted with the latest sports magazine but finally replied, "Yup! *And* I'm going to make the basketball team at my new school!"

Isaiah pretended to spin a basketball on his pointer finger and laughed; nudging his little sister in the ribs to cheer-up.

"*HA HA HA*! Stop it Isaiah! *HA HA HA*! OK-OK! Mercy! MERCY!" Niyah laughed, quickly forgetting the memories of their old apartment still broadcasting in her mind.

Isaiah *loved* sports but was also on the chess team, art club, and editor of the newspaper at his old middle school. Isaiah was *so* popular, someone could have started a club about *him*. Niyah thought her brother was the *coolest* of cool; maybe it was his shoulder-length dreadlocks or his checkerboard fingerless-driving gloves that gave him great confidence. Just like Niyah's compass, Isaiah's gloves *never* left his side. He always wore them to avoid blistering his hands from his wheelchair, which he used more like a skateboard considering all the tricks he was always learning to do. Many tried to judge Isaiah because he couldn't walk but the Zuri family never believed for a single moment that using a wheelchair would stop Isaiah from accomplishing *anything* he wanted in life.

The car began to slow down and Niyah straightened up in her seat; straining her neck to make sense of the blurry images of houses and signs, until the car eventually stopped. Cautiously leaning over her brother, she looked out of the opposite window and couldn't believe her eyes.

"Ok guys, here we are, 23 Lotus Drive," announced Mr. Zuri.

"I just love the name of our new road," Mrs. Zuri said as she searched for her umbrella in the passenger seat door. "Even the Lotus flower grows in the muddy waters but it still manages to reach *above* the surface to stretch its petals in the sun's rays."

Niyah sat for a minute thinking of her mom's words then zipped up her teal rain coat and jumped out of the car leaping right into a massive puddle; she was too distracted to notice.

SPLASH!

She stared up at her lemon-color house with its dark green shutters, beautiful flowerbed that wrapped around the entire front yard, and basketball hoop above the garage. The front porch had three steps and a ramp, which led to a dark mahogany wood door. Focusing her eyes, Niyah noticed a bronze door knocker in the shape of a lion's head mounted on the door; its mouth stretched wide.

"I dare any visitor to reach the handle hanging from those roaring clenches," thought Niyah.

Just then, she heard a faint yelling in the distance.

"Perrooo!"

She looked around but didn't see anyone else outside other than her family.

"Niyah! Let's get inside before you catch a cold," shouted Mrs. Zuri as she grabbed Niyah's hand and the two made a sprint to the front porch.

Mr. Zuri helped Isaiah out of the car and he quickly sped for the ramp on the porch, attempting to dash through the raindrops with every twist of his wheels.

"Wheeley, wheeley, wheeley!" chanted Niyah from the porch, pumping her fist in the air as Isaiah shifted his weight and spun on his left wheel.

"Be careful Isaiah!" shouted their mom, accidentally cracking a smile at her wild kids; Niyah still fist pumping as Isaiah was coming up the ramp backwards (of course).

As the Zuri family entered their home for the first time, a warm calm filled inside Niyah. She remembered how long they lived in a tiny apartment while her parents worked hard to save for a house and this was it, the day had *finally* come. Looking around the empty space, she released the anxious feeling in the pit of her stomach and embraced the name of her new street.

"Lotus Drive, the <u>Empress</u> has arrived."

2

CATCHING PERRO

Niyah's eyes shot open as her alarm clock boomed with music at 6 AM. She reached over to her nightstand, slapped her turtle clock off, and exhaled in the relief of silence.

SIGH!

She accidentally set her alarm for AM instead of PM; the time she *meant* to search for a good star gazing point with her telescope. Niyah took another deep breath and closed her eyelids slowly…

Niyah dreamed that she was flying over the earth's galaxy, the Milky Way, watching the billions of stars twinkling in the deep purple atmosphere. Then she was floating over the red planet Mars, carefully curving around its two moons.

"Time for some high-speed fun," she thought.

Niyah pushed the speed-of-sound button on her jet-pack to soar to our neighboring galaxy, Andromeda; its stars totaling in the trillions. She briefly drifted in awe as she witnessed a supernova exploding in the distance but its shock waves forced her further away...

"Niyah," called a distant voice from the kitchen.

Niyah went rushing past the outline of North America, finally slowing down by using reverse thrust on her jet-pack...

"NIY-AAAH!" screamed Isaiah.

Niyah opened her eyes, pushed her elbows against her bed, and sat up. She scratched her head as she looked around her new room; her curls sticking up in all directions as a result of her wild space exploration. Niyah's room was filled with moving boxes labeled: *Gear, Music, Board Games, Art Supplies,* and *Clothes* but only the *Gear* box had been opened. Her *Gear* box was one of the largest in her room and it stored some of Niyah's most prized possessions including her telescope, flashlight, safety rope, camera, binoculars, and backpack.

The smell of breakfast drifted up Niyah's nose, making her stomach grumble.

GRRRRRrrrrrrrr

"Time to eat," she thought.

Niyah hopped off her bed, put on her comfy peacock slippers, and headed downstairs.

"That must have been a good dream," said Mrs. Zuri, as Niyah walked into the kitchen and sat down at the table.

"Yes, it was mom..." replied Niyah, "...thanks a lot *morning* bird," she quickly added (glaring at her brother).

"My bad," chuckled Isaiah; with a mouth full of eggs.

"Mmm hmm," said Niyah, her stern face fading into a grin. Niyah chewed her food as she listened to Isaiah describe how he heard a mysterious dog howling during the night.

"There I was, having my weekly dream about <u>Michael Jordan</u> training me for college ball, when *suddenly,* I was startled from my *blissful* sleep. Some *annoying* dog was howling outside, over and over and over and over and-"

"Ok, we get it Isaiah," said Niyah laughing.

"*Anyway,* when I looked out the window, I saw a small white dog with spots but then it ran into the woods behind the house," finished Isaiah, as he commenced stuffing his face with eggs *and* pancakes *simultaneously*.

"AAAAA-OOOOOOHHHH," he howled through his stuffed mouth, sending bits of eggs flying across the table.

"Isaiah! Get a hold of yourself," said Mrs. Zuri.

"Yes, ma'am," Isaiah quickly replied and continued to chew his food; managing to secretly flash his sister a see-food smile.

Niyah laughed as she put her dishes in the sink and thanked her mom for breakfast. After cleaning her plate, she sprinted upstairs to get dressed, brush her teeth, wash her face, and *fix* her hair. When she was done, she grabbed her trusty compass, camera, and flashlight, threw them in her backpack and hurried downstairs.

"ByemomI'mgoingoutside" Niyah said, so quickly that it all sounded like *one* word.

"OK Honey but stay close, no wandering off," her mom replied.

"So many new things to discover," thought Niyah, as she jumped off her porch into her lawn and down to the sidewalk.

Further down Lotus Drive, Niyah could see two boys yelling at each other. One of them was wearing a white t-shirt, grey camouflage shorts, and black skater sneakers. He had straight brown hair down to his shoulders and a pair of black sunglasses hanging from the collar of his shirt.

"Those look exactly like dad's sunglasses," thought Niyah, as she walked further downhill.

The other boy wore a light blue polo shirt with a lion patch over the heart, plaid shorts, and white high-top basketball sneakers. His hair was short and spiky and looked like it could cut your hand if you dare touched it.

"He SURE loves gel!" she thought, finally approaching close enough to understand their shouting.

"<u>Donde es mi</u> <u>PERRO</u>?"

"How would I know where your dog is?"

"YOU were taking him for a walk!"

"<u>YO-NO- SÉ</u>!"

Niyah realized they were speaking a combination of English *and* Spanish as she interrupted their heated debate.

"Hi guys, I'm Niyah," she said, giving a fearless wave at them both.

The boys stopped yelling, turning to see who dared to disturb their screaming match. For a minute they simply looked at Niyah: her smiling face and dimples, curly brown hair, purple reggae festival t-shirt, jeans, and teal-glitter sneakers.

The spiky-haired boy began to blush but the other finally spoke up.

"What's up, I'm Miguel…and *this* is my twin brother Hugo," Hugo gave a wave.

"Nice to meet you; I just moved to 23 Lotus….ummm, what were you guys shouting about?" asked Niyah looking from Miguel to Hugo, who finally found his voice and replied.

"Our dog, Perro. He ran away last night when I took him on his walk. My brother thinks *I'm* hiding him on purpose," Hugo explained.

"I know you did something with my Perro, so just TELL ME!" demanded Miguel, glaring at his brother.

"Oh, was that *your* dog barking last night?" asked Niyah.

"You heard a dog barking?" asked the twins in <u>unison</u>.

"Yes, I mean, *I* didn't but my brother said there was a white dog with spots barking outside his window last night and that it ran into the woods," explained Niyah as she bent down to tie her loose shoe lace.

"Then *into* the woods we go! Come on Hugo, I will use you as a shield against giant spiders that decide to attack," said Miguel laughing and pushing his brother to walk but Hugo looked scared.

"Bu-Bu-But I don't want to go into the woods," stammered Hugo, "Mrs. Angelou says its *haunted.*"

"Don't be silly," interrupted Niyah, pointing a finger toward the woods declaring, "In the words of <u>President F.D.R.</u>, "There is nothing to fear but fear itself!'"

Looking both confused and inspired, Hugo had a change of heart and followed his brother and Niyah behind their house, across the backyard, and into the woods. The forest was deep; the trees went as far back as the eye could see. The ground was covered with dried up leaves left over from the past winter and the creepy silence was broken every now-and-then with sounds of twigs crunching under their feet as they made their way in.

"PEEEERRRRRRRRRROOOOOOOO!" screamed Miguel, "WHERE ARE YOU BOY? WE'RE HERE TO RESCUE YOU!"

"We don't even know where we're going," said Hugo raising and dropping his arms at his sides, "We could be walking in circles!"

"Well, I can take care of that," said Niyah and she took off her backpack, searched around inside, and pulled out her compass.

"OK, so…according to my compass we are walking south west. My house faces east, I checked in my room before I went to bed, so let's keep walking in *this* direction for a while."

The twins exchanged eye contact quickly, they were impressed. They followed behind Niyah as she led the way, and the three of them continued to call out for the dog.

"So why did you name your dog, *dog*?" Niyah asked, as they walked over broken tree limbs and large rocks.

"You speak *Spanish*?" asked Miguel.

"A little, I like to learn different languages," replied Niyah, as she stepped over a broken branch in her path.

"Well, we couldn't think of a name for him, so we thought, why not just name him 'dog' in Spanish; that's how we came up with Perro," said Miguel.

"That *is* practical," replied Niyah, as they walked under an abandoned tire swing suspended high up. The rope holding the tire was worn down and looked as if it would come crashing down at any minute.

SNAP!

"Did you hear that? Shhhh!" said Niyah, bending low to the ground and scanning the forest with her eyes.

SNAP!

"Over there!" whispered Hugo.

In the distance they could see a little white blur moving around a large tree trunk. They slowly crawled on the ground to get closer; in case it was Perro they did not want to scare him off but in case it wasn't Perro they could run for their lives.

"It's him! Perrrooo!" shouted Miguel and he jumped up onto his feet, his armed stretched open. The dog looked up at Miguel and then began running back east; the *opposite* direction.

"Quick, catch him!" said Niyah and the three began to run after Perro, dodging low-hanging tree branches and hopping over shallow puddles.

"Hugo, do you still have his leash?" shouted Miguel as they ran, "Yeah!" replied Hugo, as he pulled it out of his back pocket to show his brother. Before they realized it, they were out of the woods, running through Niyah's backyard, and within snatching distance to Perro.

"Okay, on the count of three, me and Miguel will grab Perro and Hugo, you put on his leash!" shouted Niyah.

"Let's do iiiiiiiiittttttt!" yelled Hugo.

"ONE, TWO, THREE!" shouted Niyah and she jumped forward grabbing Perro's back legs and Miguel catching hold of Perro's body.

Hugo hooked the leash and still holding on to it announced, "I did iiittttttttt!"

Looking down at Niyah and Miguel covered in dirt and grass stains he quickly re-stated, "I mean- *We* did it!" and they all started laughing.

Picking out twigs from their hair and holding on *tight* to Perro's leash, the three of them sat in Niyah's backyard talking until the sun began to set. Niyah shared some of her classic adventure stories with the twins; Hugo and Miguel *oohing* and *ahhing* with all the bold details. In return, they told Niyah *all* about the neighborhood and her new school Xavier Elementary; the twins were the same age as Niyah, so there was a chance they would be in the same class. Then, Niyah listened for what felt like a <u>century</u> as Miguel went into <u>strategic</u> detail explaining how he was precisely one minute and 17 seconds older than Hugo, which in *his* mind meant he was the older brother.

"I despise these – *accusations* Mr. Gonzales. You know I'm the firstborn!" Hugo replied furiously.

"Why does it even matter? You guys are *twins,* do you understand how COOL that is?" asked Niyah; mediating her first-ever Gonzales feud.

The twins looked at Niyah with a dazed expression; no one *ever* made perfect sense to them before.

"It *doesn't* matter-sorry Hugo," said Miguel smirking, "You know I love you like a brother."

"That's because I *am* your brother," Hugo said as he laughed.

Just then, Perro began howling *miserably*. Maybe he was hungry or simply had enough excitement for one day. Niyah didn't want to miss her star gazing opportunity so she stood up to head inside.

"<u>Kwaheri</u> guys," said Niyah as she brushed off the leaves stuck to her jeans.

"Uhhhhh, come again?" asked Miguel, attempting to decipher Niyah's *secret* alien language as he stood up.

"It means bye in Swahili, I figured you guys want to know some of my language too. Don't you want more wrinkles?" said Niyah.

"Wrinkles? No *way*! I don't want to end up like Old Man Bernie down the street, HE LOOKS LIKE HE'S 400 YEARS OLD!" hollered Hugo, as he squished Perro's face in demonstration (Perro slobbering all over Hugo's hands).

"Not on your face, in your *brain*. Every time you learn something new, you get a wrinkle in your brain," finished Niyah, as she opened the back door of her house.

"Oh, well in that case, Kwaheri Niyah," said Hugo, as he surrendered to Perro's drool, wiping the extreme excess off on his shorts. The twins walked home, two houses down, as Niyah stepped inside.

"I'm home!" she announced.

"There's my girl, did you have a good day?" asked Mr. Zuri, who was sitting in the living room watching the evening news and sipping a cup of <u>chai tea</u>.

"It was great dad!" she replied, hurtling herself on the couch and telling him all about the twins and helping them find their dog Perro.

"Seems like things are off to a great start Niyah! Now don't forget to wash those adventurous-covered hands," said Mr. Zuri, giving his grass-stained daughter a big hug.

Niyah ran upstairs to scrub her hands and quickly use her telescope before dinner. She studied the sky almost every night, determined to master navigation using the stars and moon alone. She took her telescope out of her *Gear* box and placed it in front of her window; she turned its knobs to focus on the crater-face moon and then stared at the North Star sparkling in the sky.

"Good Evening <u>Polaris</u>, you're very bright tonight...actually, the whole sky is brighter...THANK YOU suburbs," she thought; Niyah was never able to see the stars so brightly with all the city lights in her old neighborhood.

Wanting to see the full constellation of the little dipper, she lowered her telescope and zoomed out. Accidentally, she noticed a little face staring out of an upstairs bedroom in the house directly across the street from her. All of a sudden, the light in that room went out and pink curtains were drawn across the windows.

3

THE PINE MACHINE

The weeks seemed to fly by now that Niyah made new friends. It was already the last weekend of summer break and she had *so* much fun that she completely forgot none of her old friends kept in touch. Niyah and the Gonzales twins had a new expedition almost every day and were upset that it had to end. Over the summer, they helped Mrs. Angelou at 40 Lotus Drive clean out her garage for a tag sale (resulting in an <u>unforeseen</u> attack by a family of pigeons when they moved her old television from a dark corner of the garage), they constructed a "waterpark" out of five different slip-and-slides in the twins' backyard, mastered locating several constellations using Niyah's telescope, and finally managed to give Perro a *decent* bath.

The first day of school started like any normal day for Niyah. She had breakfast with her family, packed her backpack for the day, met Hugo and Miguel outside, but *then* the three walked to school for the very first time.

"Are you nervous Niyah?" asked Hugo, as they walked towards the red brick building in the distance.

"No," she replied, "but I hope we're in the same class."

"Me too," said the twins in unison (they had a habit of doing that).

Up ahead they saw a girl wearing pink from head to toe walking towards the school. As they passed her, Niyah tried to introduce herself, "Hi, I'm Niyah."

The girl didn't reply, instead, she walked faster to dodge them; her pink backpack flapping left to right as she half-sprinted.

Flip-flap, flip-flap, flip-flap!

"What's up with *Runaway Girl*?" asked Niyah, looking slightly hurt.

"Oh, that's just Mihn, don't let her bother you-she's *never* talked to *us* either," said Miguel, as the crossing guard directed them to the other side of the street.

"Xavier Elementary," Niyah read aloud, as they walked under the school's navy blue and yellow sign and entered through its double doors. The lobby was *filled* with kids unsure of where to go, kindergarteners crying after their parents, and teachers *trying* to keep all the chaos in order.

"This way," said Hugo, and Niyah followed the twins through the crowd, making a slight left turn to a quiet section of classrooms, where a man stood waiting to greet them.

"Names?" asked the teacher, who they could now see had an enormous mustache that curled at both ends.

"We're the Gonzales brothers," stated Miguel and the teacher quickly scanned the list of names on the clipboard and then replied, "Oh, yes, Hugo and Miguel Gonzales? You will be in my classroom this year, room 285."

"Thanks," said Hugo and the twins gave Niyah a thumbs up for good luck as they walked into their classroom.

"And you Miss?" heard Niyah, as she watched her friends walking away.

"I'm Niyah, Niyah Zuri," she said, finally coming back to reality.

"What - an - *interesting* name..." replied the teacher, twisting one end of his curly mustache as he examined Niyah and *not* the classroom list.

"It means beautiful purpose," said Niyah; adults *always*

asked her what it meant.

"How *fascinating*! And in what language would that be?" he asked, now twisting the other end of his mustache, as he prepared a mental list of interview questions for Niyah. However, he was shortly interrupted by four more kids asking for their classroom number.

"Miss Zuri, I'll save my inquiries for *another* day, now let's see…here we are," he said, running his finger down the classroom list until he found her name, "Classroom 287."

Niyah's heart sank; she was not going to be in class with her only friends but thanked the teacher and walked into her homeroom. Suddenly there was a comforting voice announcing, "Good Morning class, I'm your teacher Mrs. Ridley, please, have a seat!"

Mrs. Ridley was smiling kindly and was wearing teal colored glasses (Niyah's favorite color). Niyah could feel the joy rising inside her again and decided she was going to make the best of her new class and catch up with the twins during recess. She stood at the front of the room searching for the perfect desk: The classroom was fairly large with five rows of four desks taking up most of the space. Niyah couldn't help but notice that the desks seemed to be from different <u>decades:</u> some had mint-green seats and desktops while others were made of stainless steel with a polished blue plastic seat. She noticed a unique desktop that opened to reveal a secret storage compartment and quickly sat down before anyone else could claim it.

"Hello Class, as I said before, my name is Mrs. Ridley, and I am your fourth-grade homeroom teacher. We will learn *plenty* of interesting things this year as we explore - (Niyah's attention sharpened as she heard the word *explore*) history, math, science, and reading. But today, let's learn about one another, starting with attendance."

Mrs. Ridley pulled out a sheet from her red folder and began calling out names, her voice drifting into the background as Niyah looked out the classroom windows. Niyah could see a big playground with three slides, eight swings, a basketball court, baseball field, and soccer field.

"Niyah Zuri?" called Mrs. Ridley.

"Present," said Niyah as she whipped her head around quickly; her and Mrs. Ridley exchanged smiles.

"Mihn Li?" Mrs. Ridley called.

"Here," said a girl, sitting to the right of Niyah.

Mihn Li quickly peaked over at Niyah. Her hair was in two pigtails tied with pink bows and she was wearing a light pink polka dot dress with dark pink stockings. This was all topped off with a pair of hot pink glasses and glitter pink sneakers.

"That's a whooole lot of pink!" thought Niyah, looking back at her classmate. Noticing they both liked shimmering sneakers, she attempted to introduce herself again.

"Nice kicks," said Niyah and to her surprise Mihn smiled and replied, "Thanks, I like yours too."

Shocked, Niyah wanted to ask Mihn why she ignored her and whether she lives in the house across the street with the pink curtains. If she did, Niyah needed to know why Mihn stared at her house almost every night but before Niyah could say another word the teacher asked for the everyone's attention. The class spent the next three hours playing geography games until it was time for recess. Mrs. Ridley opened the back door and watched 99% of the class run out onto the playground. Niyah grabbed her backpack, peeking quickly inside to check her gear and then followed the rest of the class outside. Niyah saw Mihn standing alone but as she walked up to her to have another chat the twins spotted her from across the playground.

"Ni-YYYUUUUUAAAAHHHH!" they hollered walking towards her.

She waved at Miguel and Hugo and then turned around to invite Mihn to meet them but she quickly interrupted Niyah's invitation.

"Ewww, you talk to *boys*?" her faced screwed up tight in judgment.

"Yeah! They're my FRIENDS!" Niyah could feel her ears getting hot; the pulsing in her veins clouded her hearing, causing her to shout more loudly than normal.

As quick as the wind, Mihn turned on the spot and walked off in the other direction.

Confused about what just happened, Niyah turned to meet up with the twins, rubbing the tips of her ears as she walked.

"Hey guys, what's up?" asked Niyah, her ears still flushed red from irritation.

"Was Mihn *actually* talking to you?" asked Miguel, his eyes wide open in shock.

"Yup, but I guess she doesn't want to be friends with *boys*," replied Niyah. "*Anyways*, what's your class like? Is your teacher nice? And what's with his *mustache*?" Niyah asked, finally cracking a smile.

They made their way around the playground as Niyah listened to the Gonzales twins describe their teacher and some of their classmates, going into *great* detail about a kid named Ernie who spent the whole morning eating his earwax. The twins even made up a fairy tale where Sir Ernie rode upon a horse and used a slingshot to strike his enemies with earwax pellets to defend the kingdom.

"Gross!" said Niyah, squeezing her face between her hands to stop from laughing.

They grabbed a red kickball from an open crate and walked towards the soccer field but before they could start up a game Hugo kicked it *far* across the field; the ball rolling under a nearby pine tree.

"WHOOPS!" said Hugo, as Niyah and Miguel shook their heads laughing.

"No worries, come on, let's go get it," said Niyah.

They walked across the soccer field and stopped at the third pine tree to their right. It was a *very* tall pine tree with long swopping branches, making it difficult to see the kickball.

"Where did it go?" asked Miguel, stooping down low to look under the extensive branches, "I can't see it under there."

"I can take care of that!" said Niyah, as she took off her backpack and began to dig for something; the twins were use to Niyah being prepared for adventure.

"Here we go," said Niyah, as she whipped out her flashlight.

CLICK!

Niyah turned the flashlight on and bent down low to shine the light under the shaded pine tree but she still couldn't see anything.

"We'll have to go under the branches," said Niyah, as she crawled into the unknown.

Hugo and Miguel shrugged their shoulders then held up a bottom branch as they all made their way in. Niyah and the twins were always ready to discover something new but what they found beneath the sweeping branches surprised them all. Before their very eyes were kick balls of all sizes (including their own), rusty model airplanes hanging from random branches high above the ground, a bright green reclining chair, stacks of old newspapers, some dusty clothes, and tons of odds and ends scattered *all* over the place. Their mouths dropped wide open in shock, not one of them able to say any real words.

W-O-A-H

The crew walked around under the pine tree trying to figure out where all these things came from and to whom it all belonged. Strangely, they couldn't see any of these things from outside the tree.

"Hey! This could be our club house!" said Miguel, as he opened a yellow umbrella and a dozen gold coins poured on his head, "Ow! During recess, I mean."

"Yeah," said Hugo, as he flipped a metal ping-pong paddle in his hand, posing as if he was in a Table Tennis Championship game.

"And what do we have here?" said Niyah, as she unrolled an old map that was tucked behind a stack of newspapers. She squinted to read a handwritten timeline along the bottom.

"1492, June 1908, Spring of 1776, *Tri-as-sic*, <u>Triassic period</u>...," she pronounced under her breath.

"What do you think all these dates are for?" asked Niyah, as she spread the map open on the ground and the twins walked over to inspect it. In the upper right-hand corner of the map were letters that seemed to be initials: A.R., P.D., and K.V.

"*What could these letters mean?*" thought Niyah, pressing her lips together as she examined the old <u>parchment</u>.

"Hmmm, this timeline is funny... there's a lot of a space between the dates, like it wasn't finished," said Miguel, scanning the map with his eyes.

"Hey, look at that," Hugo added, pointing to a sentence written in the upper left corner of the map.

They strained their necks over the map and narrowed their eyes to read the faded writing out loud.

"TO SOLVE PAST MYSTERIES, TRUE SEEKERS OF KNOWLEDGE NEED YOU BE, THEN YOU CAN UNLOCK THE SECRETS OF HISTORY BUT YOU MUST USE THE POWER OF THREE"

There was a *sudden* flash of light.

 NIYAH ZURI & THE PHARAOH'S THRONE

4

NOT JURASSIC, TRIASSIC

"Where…"

breath

"are…"

breath

"we?" panted Niyah, as she tried to catch her breath and get up on her feet.

"I don't know, it looks like we're in the *jungle*," said Miguel, now standing to help Hugo up.

There they stood; in the middle of the _wilderness._ There were overgrown trees towering almost 70 feet tall and plants with leaves the size of high schoolers. The climate was both hot and dry, making them all sweat uncontrollably.

"This-is-COOL!" shouted Hugo, his voice startling a group of mysterious-looking flying reptiles that fluttered up through the canopy of branches above their heads.

"Shhh! We don't want to call attention to ourselves; we don't even know where we _are_!" Niyah said quietly, as she studied the map still clutched in her hand with the flashlight. The twins were rotating around in circles, slowly staring at all the flora and fauna around them, when Niyah interrupted, "OK, let's think, what _exactly_ happened?"

"_Well_, we were looking at the map in the club house…" started Miguel, "…and then _I_ pointed to some words on the map and the three of us read that rhyme…" continued Hugo, "…and then there was a _burst_ of light, everything went dark, and when we opened our eyes we were in the _middle_ of the _jungle_," finished Niyah.

"Hey, do you think we…we…ummm…what's it called again…teleported?" asked Miguel snatching the map from Niyah's tight grip.

"_Maybe_ but where did we teleport _to_?" asked Hugo snatching the map from his brother to swat away a gargantuan mosquito.

"Wait a minute!" said Niyah and she carefully peeled Hugo fingers off the map and unrolled it on the jungle ground.

"Before we read that incantation, I was reading this timeline out loud...not in order though...I think the last date I said was 'Triassic period'," stated Niyah, as she casually nudged away a centipede crawling across the map.

"Hold on, Triassic? You mean like... *Jurassic*?" asked Hugo.

"Miguel, remember the movie we watched with Tio Francisco about the dinosaurs chasing after humans in the..." Hugo's voice suddenly became quiet and his eyes widened as he looked at Niyah and his brother.

"...*Jungle*." Niyah whispered in realization.

They looked at each other in disbelief then all around them at the mysterious forest. There were large lizards with fin-like spikes along their backs walking slowly along the ground, bright colored insects that appeared to be dragonflies zooming by in all directions, salamanders crawling along the trunks of trees, and a group of birds could be heard in the distance screeching loudly (probably the *same* flying-reptiles Hugo scared away).

"We have to make sure, let's take a look around" whispered Niyah, as she tied her hair back in a ponytail and whipped out her compass.

Niyah wondered what the map possessed to make time travel possible, "*Is it some sort of portal?*"

They made their way through the *mysterious* jungle, <u>analyzing</u> the long vines hovering over the heads, and listening to the *eerie* sounds echoing around them. Niyah's compass guided them further into the deep woods; twisting and turning through what seemed to be a never-ending maze. It didn't seem possible but the trees appeared to be getting taller the further they walked and every sound made their ears perk up in caution. Even time began to blend together in a haze: a group of dragonflies zooming by Niyah's face, Miguel accidentally stepping on a snail, Niyah checking her compass, Hugo thinking he heard the birds he startled earlier coming back to strike, Miguel saying it was hot, Niyah checking her compass, Hugo wiping his face...

Dragonflies, snails, compass, birds, the heat, compass, sweat...

Dragonflies (*are those the same ones?*) ...

Snails (*how many of these things are out here?*) ...

Compass (*is this thing even working?*) ...

Birds (*please don't get me!*) ...

The heat (*I-need-water*) ...

Compass (*wait, I thought we were going South?*) ...

Sweat (*waterrrr*) …

Dragonflies (*they almost flew into my MOUTH!*) …

Snails (*AGAIN?!*) …

Compass (*hold on, how are we going WEST?!*)

Birds (*I'm really SORRY!*)

The heat (*MUST…GET…WATER!*)

Compass (*ARE YOU SERIOUS?!*)

Sweat (*WATER!!!*) …

Just then, a rustling sound could be heard from behind them; Niyah and the twins stiffened their bodies and held their breath. What appeared to be a small fury mouse ran across their trail; the rodent *also* pausing for a moment to analyze the foreigners in its track.

"I feel like we're searching for Perro…for the *100th time*! What's up with *us* and the *woods*?" asked Miguel, using the bottom of his shirt to wipe his sweaty forehead.

"Good question Bro," added Hugo, using his sleeve to wipe the gel now leaking down the side of his face.

"Hey, check it out! Over *there*!" said Niyah, pointing to an opening near some tall plants.

They made their way through the last stretch of jungle;

each step more slippery than the next due to the moss-covered ground. Finally reaching the end of their path, they pulled several *enormous* leaves to one side. Their six little eyes peaked out of the shady jungle but what they saw before them they *couldn't* believe. Lurking around, as tall as some of the trees, were *dinosaurs*.

GASP!

One of the dinosaurs turned its body towards the noise and the three ducked down quickly behind the large plant.

"What are we going to do?" whispered Hugo, his sweaty-face stricken with horror, "We've got to get out of here!"

"I know, I know, I'm thinking…." said Niyah, scanning the map with her flashlight for any clues. The <u>humidity</u> was blurring her vision; she wiped her eyes with the collar of her shirt, and quickly continued examining the map for a way out.

Boom…

They could feel the vibrations of the dinosaur; it was walking *towards* them.

"OK, let's read the rhyme again together and *hope* it will get us back home, wait for my signal," said Niyah and the twins nodded their head.

Boom…boom…

The vibrations were getting faster, the dinosaur was getting *closer*.

"We need to get back to the club house...*club house... club house!*" said Niyah, as she squeezed her eyes tight imagining the pine tree club house filled with all its junk. Then, she opened her eyes, gave the twins a nod, and pointed at the sentence in the corner of the map.

"TO SOLVE PAST MYSTERIES..."

BOOM...BOOM...

"...TRUE SEEKERS OF KNOWLEDGE NEED YOU BE, THEN YOU CAN UNLOCK THE SECRETS OF HISTORY..."

BOOM, BOOM, BOOM, BOOM...

"... BUT YOU MUST USE THE POWER OF THREE!"

There was a sudden *flash* of light.

5

A.R. REVEALED

Niyah, Miguel, and Hugo lay on the ground of the club house, their eyes closed tightly and their bodies stiff afraid to move. One-by-one they opened their eyes and to their relief saw they made it back safely. They jumped to their feet shouting, "We did it! We did it!" giving each other fist bumps and high fives. Niyah attempted to do the moonwalk but the dirt surface was not smooth enough; the twins did the robot.

A whistle blew loudly in the distance.

"Recess is done, we better go!" announced Miguel.

Niyah folded the map and tucked it under the cushion of the green recliner for safe keeping. Realizing she must have looked like a sweaty mess, Niyah searched in her backpack for a something to wipe her muggy face; an embroidered handkerchief did the trick. Next, she removed her hair tie and shook her head wildly, allowing her curls to fall into place, then followed the twins out from under the pine tree.

"Do you guys realize what just *happened* to us?!" asked Niyah, as they ran across the soccer field and back up to the school.

"Yeah, we teleported, and it was A-M-A-Z-I-N-G!" said Miguel, as he threw his arms up towards the sky. "The map was some kind of key," he finished, kicking the red ball to his brother.

"Listen," demanded Niyah, as she stopped in her tracks; the twins turning around to face her.

"We can't tell *anyone* about the map *or* the club house, they seem to be linked together. Someone could get hurt and until we figure out *how* it works, it's not *safe* to spread the news," she explained. Niyah's face was serious but she had a twinkle in her eyes; the twins knew it was her love for adventure.

"That's a good point," said Hugo, "So let's make a pact, a promise to keep this secret between us three."

"I promise," said Miguel and Niyah responded, "Me too."

They looked at each other in agreement then turned to keep walking back towards the school. There was one kid still outside on the basketball court practicing his layups and dribbling; he quickly looked their direction but continued with his basketball drills.

"So, what are we going to *call* ourselves, you know, now that we can *time* travel and all?" asked Hugo, as he rubbed his chin.

"How about the *TIME* Travelers?" asked Miguel.

"*TOO* obvious," answered Hugo.

"OK then, you figure out a name *genius*," said Miguel as they finally made it to the playground and walked past the rusty slides.

"Hmmm…how about…*TIME* Stoppers?" asked Hugo.

"And THAT'S not obvious?" snickered Miguel.

Listening to the Gonzales brothers argue was like watching a tennis match; Niyah would turn her head to one brother then turn to the other, and back and forth, and back and forth. She realized she had to referee this match quickly or risk a *serious* neck cramp.

"How about we keep our own names and figure out what

we want to *discover* instead?" asked Niyah.

"Makes sense," replied the twins in unison as they reached their separate classroom doors. Niyah noticed just then that Mrs. Ridley had been watching them walk back *curiously* from the classroom window.

"See you after school," said Hugo, as he and his brother walked back into their classroom and Niyah turned away into hers. She sat down at her desk and put her backpack on the floor, taking a moment to sit perfectly still to quiet her mind. Unexpectedly, something caught Niyah's eye: it was Mrs. Ridley's satchel leaning against the desk on the floor. The satchel was made of caramel-color leather and there was something stitched on the side of the strap that looked familiar to Niyah but she needed a *closer* look.

"Alright class, everyone take out a piece of paper and write down five jobs you may want to have when you grow up," instructed Mrs. Ridley. "Remember, you can do anything you set your mind to, so be creative!" she added before sitting back at her desk to sort through a red folder stuffed with loose papers.

Quickly, Niyah rummaged through her backpack for a pencil and walked to the front of the class to the sharpener; *right* next to Mrs. Ridley's desk. It seemed as though Mrs. Ridley ignored Niyah on purpose as she took her time sharpening her *already* sharp pencil. Looking down at Mrs. Ridley's briefcase, she could finally read the monogram stitched on the briefcase: *A.R.* She sat back down at her desk wondering why those initials were so familiar to her.

"A.R. ... A.R. ..." she thought.

After a minute or so, Niyah decided to take out a piece of paper and begin working on the assignment given.

"Archeologist, Marine Biologist, Treasure Hunter..." she wrote; trying to remember to dot all her i's and cross all her t's just as her father always reminded her when reviewing homework.

Niyah's thoughts were swept into a daydream about the hidden club house and mysterious map. She began doodling the wild rainforest scene while it was still fresh in her mind on the bottom of her assignment. Niyah sketched <u>colossal</u> trees, draped in ropes of vines, lizard-like birds soaring in the air, and the twins racing on the backs of dinosaurs as Niyah examined a massive dinosaur egg with an oversized magnifying glass.

"No one would believe it," she thought, shaking her head as she remembered the ancient jungle's <u>intricate</u> details and how a dinosaur almost ate her and the twins as a tasty snack.

Suddenly, Niyah snapped back into reality: she remembered where she saw the initials on Mrs. Ridley's briefcase.

"The same initials A.R. are on the map in the club house," thought Niyah, as she blinked quickly; her mind processing this final puzzle piece.

"But if Mrs. Ridley is A.R., then that means…"

Niyah glanced up from writing; Mrs. Ridley was staring *right* at her.

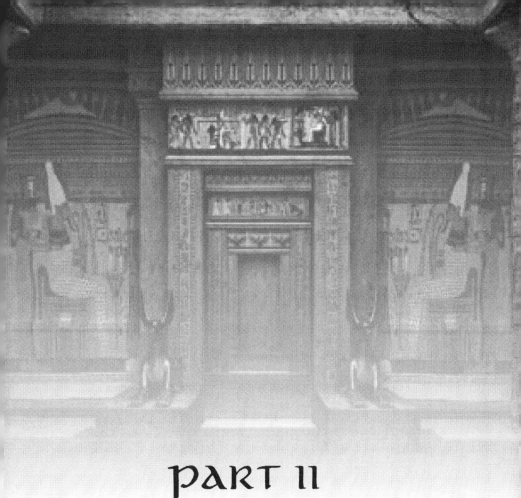

PART II

ASCENDING THE THRONE

6

MISSION ACCEPTED

"Mrs. Ridley is A.R.! Those are her initials on our map!" Niyah said excitedly, as her and the Gonzales twins walked home from their first day of school.

"Niyah, are you sure? Just because she has the same initials doesn't mean she knows about the clubhouse *or* the map," asked Miguel.

"Don't you guys *remember*? She was watching us *very* curiously when we walked back from the Pine machine and *then*, when I noticed the initials on her briefcase, she started *staring* at me…as if she could *read my mind*," said Niyah, wiggling her fingers over her head.

"I'm telling you, Mrs. Ridley is A.R.!" urged Niyah, as they stopped at the corner of the street and waited for the crossing guard.

"*Pine* Machine - that has a nice ring to it - good one," said Hugo, completely oblivious to the rest of Niyah's discovery.

"Thanks Hugo," said Niyah, shaking her head chuckling.

"Maybe we should ask her for some advice?" suggested Miguel, as the crossing guard escorted them across the street.

"That's *exactly* what I was thinking," said Niyah, as she pulled her compass out of her pocket and focused on the <u>coordinates</u> back to Lotus Drive. "We just need to figure out *how* to talk to her...we can't be *too* excited or she'll think we're not *mature* enough but we can't be too *serious* or she'll think we're not *interested* in discovering history..." mumbled Niyah, as she weighed the plan carefully in her mind.

The twins exchanged looks of caution and decided to be silent as Niyah created their *master* plan; muttering to herself under her breath. They finally turned to walk down Lotus Drive, their backpacks heavy with what felt like a year's worth of homework, when Niyah bursted out, "I got it! I'll see you in the morning and explain *everything*."

"Ok, cool," said Miguel, elbowing Hugo from his vow of silence.

"OW!" reacted Hugo, "I mean, see you in the AM Niyah."

"Chao," said Niyah, as she ran up the steps onto her porch and quickly entered her house. Niyah could still hear Hugo yelling at Miguel all the way down the street, "I think you cracked my ribs!"

"Stop being such a *baby*," replied Miguel.

"Maybe I need to go to the hospital! Or MAYBE...I need to tell MOM!" threatened Hugo.

"No, don't do that bro - my arms still hurt from the last time I got in trouble and mom made me mow the lawn – it took five hours!"

Niyah shook her head and laughed as she went upstairs, announcing, "I'm home!"

"Hi Honey, how was your day," asked Mrs. Zuri.

"It was great! The twins aren't in my homeroom but we did some exploring outside during recess, Hugo had some weird adrenaline moment and kicked a ball across the *entire* soccer field, which rolled under a tree and then-" Niyah cut her sentence short, realizing she promised not to tell *anyone* about the map.

"*And*... I have a ton of homework, so I better get started, bye!" finished Niyah quickly, as she hurried in her room and slammed the door shut.

"That was close, too close," thought Niyah, as she threw her backpack on her bed and plopped down on a giant beanbag chair. Her mind started to wonder about all the places her and the twins could go using the power of the map: *the Mali Empire, the Samurai era, battles lead by Apache warrior Geronimo...*

"Oh man, my homework!" she realized, pulling herself out of daydreams.

Two hours, three math worksheets, and one reading assignment later, Niyah's mom called her downstairs for dinner.

"Mmm, that smells delicious!" said Niyah, as she entered the kitchen and helped Isaiah set the table.

"Hey," whispered Isaiah, as he passed Niyah the napkins to fold, "I can tell something's up with you. What *really* happened at school today?"

Niyah's cheeks turned pink as she tried to ignore *detective* Zuri; she could feel her brother's eyes glaring in the back of her head as she set the napkins and silverware on the table. Isaiah could read Niyah like a book and he had *ninja*-like hearing; it was hard for her to *ever* hide anything from him *so* she decided to ignore him instead.

NIYAH ZURI & THE PHARAOH'S THRONE

"Dad, you *have* to hear about the Gonzales twins' homeroom teacher, his mustache is the size of Texas!" said Niyah, as she took a seat next to her dad and hoped her brother wouldn't ask any more *curious* questions.

The Zuri family finished eating dinner and Isaiah quickly headed into his bedroom next to the living room; he wanted to finish painting some flames on his wheels before school the next day. Niyah's parents decided to watch one of their favorite TV programs Extreme Nature. Fearing more questions from Isaiah, Niyah joined them; nestling on a separate couch with a fuzzy brown blanket.

"Niyah, it's almost bedtime sweetheart; 20 minutes, then you have to head upstairs," said Mr. Zuri, wrapping an arm around his wife.

"Ok, Dad," replied Niyah, as she zoned into the show: a mountain climber was attempting to scale Mt. Everest while evading the *extreme* dangers of frostbite and starvation.

"Pete McKlowski here...I've reached Camp Two, already several days into my ascent of <u>Mt. Everest</u>," blared the TV.

The images of the mighty Mt. Everest flashed across the screen: the gusts of winds nearly blowing the climber's tent off the mountain side, the snow-capped peak he was attempting to reach, a wide-angle view of the majestic mountain...

"It's magnificent up here in the <u>Himalayas</u>; quite serene really... The people of <u>Tibet</u> call Everest 'Chomolangma' meaning

'Goddess Mother of the World' and BOY is she a beauty!"

R-I-I-I-N-G! R-I-I-I-N-G!

The sudden sound of the phone startled Niyah; her mind was deep in the show attempting to create faster routes for the mountain climber in her mind.

R-I-I-I-N-G! R-I-I-I-N-G!

"I'll get it," said Niyah, kicking off the warm blanket. She sprinted to the kitchen and slid across the smooth floor (surfer-style).

"Zuri Residence," Niyah answered.

"Niyah?"

The sound of the familiar voice gave Niyah a lump in her throat, making it hard for her to swallow.

"Niyah, listen, I know *all* about the map, I saw you three walking back from the pine trees and the drawing on your class assignment confirmed it…"

Niyah's heart began to beat faster; she could feel it pounding not only in her chest but in her ears too.

"We need to talk; *all* of us," Mrs. Ridley finished.

"I agree, we *need* to talk," replied Niyah, *finally* remembering the master plan she came up with earlier.

"I know you're A.R."

"Yes…I am."

Niyah's heart rate began to slow back down to normal and she took a deep breath before continuing.

"We need your help, we need to know if the map is safe to use," asked Niyah, twisting the phone cord over her right index finger.

"I have made a vow to guide the next generation of Xavier explorers but before I can help you three, you must agree to use the map only for the missions I assign you; *that* is the *safest* way…We shouldn't talk further over the phone, your first mission starts tomorrow. Do you agree to the terms that I've just explained?"

Niyah looked over at Isaiah's door, which was cracked open, and had a feeling that her brother was spying from his room. Just then, she heard the TV as Pete the mountain climber was videotaping another entry for his digital journal.

"If I can't do what I love, then what's my purpose?" the mountain climber asked, his voice echoing into the kitchen where Niyah stood holding the phone to her ear with both hands.

"Mission accepted," she whispered and hung up the phone.

7

PYRAMID ESCAPE

Niyah kept a close eye on her watch as she waited outside on the sidewalk for Miguel and Hugo.

Tick-tock, tick-tock, tick-tock, tick-tock....

The seconds felt like minutes, as she repeatedly tapped her foot, looked at her watch, and *strained* her neck to look down the street. Niyah was so anxious to tell the twins Mrs. Ridley called her and confirmed that she was in fact *A.R.* They would begin their first mission today during recess but she wasn't sure what sort of task Mrs. Ridley would assign them.

Eventually, Niyah saw two heads bobbling up the street towards her.

"What *took* you guys so long?" asked Niyah.

"Uhhh, it's 8:04; we're only four minutes late," answered Miguel, as he flattened his hair down on the sides.

"We had to feed Perro before we left; it was a little hard figuring out *where* he was hiding," added Hugo, who was also attempting to *repair* his hair.

"Oh, sorry…Perro must have given you a race! You guys look a mess!" said Niyah, as the three began to walk to school.

"*Tell* me about it!" said the twins in unison.

"Actually, I have some pretty big news *to* tell you. Mrs. Ridley called me last night!" said Niyah.

"WHAT?" shrieked Hugo.

"Yeah, I know; so much for needing a master plan to convince her to help us. She admitted that she's A.R. and started talking about *a vow to guide the next generation of Xavier explorers,*" answered Niyah, in her most <u>distinguished</u> voice.

"Shhh, keep your voices down," whispered Miguel, as the three of them approached the legendary Mihn Li;

fashionably pink as always.

"Hi Mihn" "Hey" "Wasssuuup" they each said in passing.

WHOOSH!

Mihn literally jumped aside at the sound of their voices - right into a group of bushes.

"Did you see her face? AAAHAHA HAHAHAHA AAAHAHAHA!" laughed Hugo, "Does she think she'll turn into a pumpkin or something if she talks to a boy?"

"I have no idea Hugo but we have bigger fish to fry- *so* about Mrs. Ridley..." said Niyah, taking a quick peek back at Mihn to make sure she was ok and then continued to <u>narrate</u> last night's *entire* call to the twins.

"Good Morning Niyah, Hugo, Miguel," welcomed the crossing guard, as he guided them across the street.

"Good Morning Mr.–Uhhh..." responded Miguel, realizing he didn't know the crossing guard's name; Niyah raised her left eyebrow up, puzzled as to *how* he knew their names in the first place.

"Vogel, Mr. Vogel. Have an *adventurous* day," he answered, walking back to his post on the opposite side of the street.

"*Adventurous* day, eh? You don't think- no, Mrs. Ridley couldn't of- *could* she?" pondered Niyah out loud; her eyebrow still at high attention.

"Don't sweat it Niyah, Mr. Vogel probably has to memorize *all* the kid's names, it's just a coincidence," said Miguel, still struggling to flatten his hair down.

"Maybe…but why would he say have an '*adventurous*' day?" stressed Niyah, as the three entered the Xavier's main doors.

"Seems to me he knows about our mission," said Hugo, who stopped to tie his sneakers in the entrance hall.

"*Exactly* what I was thinking, I guess we'll just have to wait and see. Catch you at recess," replied Niyah and they went their separate ways.

When she entered her classroom, she noticed Mrs. Ridley talking to a very tall man in a dark blue suit and gold-patterned tie.

"*That's the same man in the photograph hanging in the entrance hall of the school. It's Mr. Davis; the Principal,*" Niyah realized.

"Good Morning class," greeted Mrs. Ridley as she finally sat at her desk. "Please remember to place your homework folders in the blue tray on my desk. Now, for attendance."

Niyah's eyes followed Principal Davis as he slipped quickly out of the classroom; he didn't look back.

"Hmmm, interesting…" she thought.

As Mrs. Ridley called out the students' names for attendance, Niyah took the opportunity to be the first to submit her homework. As she placed her folder in the tray, Niyah gave Mrs. Ridley a stern head nod and walked away; somehow, she knew Mrs. Ridley understood that it meant they were ready for their first mission.

"Ok class, let's jumpstart this first week of school with multiplication review for math, a study about the earth's layers for Science…," announced Mrs. Ridley, as she wrote the week's objectives on the blackboard. "For Social Studies, we are going to learn about <u>Ancient Egypt</u> and the famous <u>King Tutankhamen</u> or King Tut for short," finished Mrs. Ridley as she passed out new worksheets.

The first student in each column of desks was handed a stack of sheets, taking one packet for themselves and passing the rest back; each student followed that order until all the worksheets were <u>distributed</u>. The next two hours dragged by: Mrs. Ridley selected a boy from the back of the classroom to read a chapter from their science books, the class had to copy notes from the blackboard, and they began their math worksheets. Niyah twirled her curly hair around her finger trying to focus on subtracting fractions but the hours were *dragging* and she couldn't stop looking up at the clock *every* two minutes. Glancing over at Mihn, she noticed a twig stuck in her hair (probably from that morning). Without saying a word, Niyah reached over and pulled the stick out; tossing it on the floor near Mihn's sneakers. Startled, Mihn glanced over at Niyah, then down at the twig and smiled.

BBBRRRIIINNNGGG!

The recess bell rang and all the kids from the homerooms ran outside. Niyah grabbed her backpack and followed her classroom out onto the playground. Her heart was beating from excitement as she approached Mrs. Ridley anxious about the details surrounding their first mission; the twins quickly spotted Niyah and made their way over.

"Hello Niyah," said Mrs. Ridley, as she watched the twins walk over, "And hello to you both: Miguel – Hugo. I want you to take this envelope; all of your instructions will be found inside. *Don't* open it until you're safely in the club house. Is that clear?"

The kids nodded their heads and Niyah took the red satin envelope, stashing it inside her backpack for safekeeping.

"Good luck," added Mrs. Ridley and walked away swiftly to settle a dispute between a group of third graders arguing over the cafeteria's secret ingredient in the nauseating pasta salad.

"It's pickle juice!" yelled one kid.

"You're w-r-o-n-g WRONG! Its Brussels sprouts!" shouted another.

"BOTH OF YOU ARE CONFUSED! I'M

ABSOLUTELY POSITIVE THAT ITS SEA URCHINS!" a different kid screamed, "And I think it's *rather* delicious."

"EEEEEEEEEWWWWWWWWWWWW!" howled the crowd surrounding the pasta salad debate.

"This is the perfect distraction, come on, let's go!" whispered Niyah and the three ran across the soccer field to the third pine tree on the right and entered. Swinging from the monkey bars, Mihn Li watched them escape under the tree.

"I wonder what they're up to?" she thought, as she hung upside down swaying her arms back and forth.

Back in the clubhouse, Niyah dug into her backpack and retrieved the envelope. She tore it open and unfolded the letter, reading it aloud: *"There are many rumors about King Tutankhamen; rumors about his life, his death, and his rise to the throne. I want you to go back in time to discover what challenge he underwent to become* <u>Pharaoh</u> *of Egypt and help him during the most* <u>critical</u> *point in his life. Travel safely in Africa's desert plains and make sure to blend in; you don't want to be spotted! Use the coordinates 1337 BC, Egypt, Africa. Safe Travels, A.R."*

"Well let's not waste any more time," said Miguel, as he stood up and started searching through the clubhouse like a mad-man; he was turning the place upside down.

"What are you looking for bro?" asked Hugo.

"What do you *think* I'm looking for? The map!" replied Miguel, now looking through a stack of old newspapers.

"*Oh*, well I put it under this chair cushion for safe keeping," responded Niyah, walking over to retrieve it. She unrolled the map carefully; spreading it open on the clubhouse ground for all to read.

"You two ready?" asked Niyah, her eyes gleaming with excitement.

"We were *born* ready! Isn't that right Hugo?" asked Miguel

"Yup! Let's *do* it!" said Hugo, giving his brother a fist bump.

Niyah took a deep breathe, exhaled slowly, and closed her eyes. She felt an excitement stirring within her but tried to remain serious as the twins waited for their queue.

"1337 B.C. Egypt, Africa," she announced and the twins joined in to read the incantation off the map.

"TO SOLVE PAST MYSTERIES, TRUE SEEKERS OF KNOWLEDGE NEED YOU BE, THEN YOU CAN UNLOCK THE SECRETS OF HISTORY BUT YOU MUST USE THE POWER OF THREE!"

FLASH!

Niyah, Hugo, and Miguel were instantly transported with a bright light through a dark tunnel that twisted and turned in all directions. None of them were prepared the first time around but *this* time they were completely alert. They could feel air wildly encompassing them and realized they were in fact floating while moving at a rapid speed. Unexpectedly, a bright light began to fill the tunnel and, just as quickly, they felt themselves *drop* to a hard surface.

OW!

OOH!

UGH!

Gradually standing, they realized they were in a dim lit room with torches hanging from dusty stone walls. Niyah dug in her backpack for her flashlight but the batteries were dead. Kicking Plan A (and her flashlight) aside, she removed a torch from the wall and began walking through a dark corridor ahead.

"Did we make it?" asked Hugo.

"Only one way to find out, come on guys!" she signaled.

As they walked, they discovered the small firelight dazzling all round them in the passageway was in fact *riches*: chests of jewels, instruments, ostrich feather fans, chariots, and swords. Niyah brought the torch closer to the wall to examine its <u>vague</u> images, which revealed intricate wall paintings of a royal ceremony.

"I think it's pretty safe to say, we made it to Egypt," concluded Miguel; looking at the <u>hieroglyphics</u> written on the walls as they continued to walk down the treasure-lined corridor.

"*Amazing*!" Niyah thought, as she carefully studied the hieroglyphics; attempting to record each image to her memory for future use.

"Yeah but *where* exactly in Egypt are we?" asked Hugo, as they reached the end of the pathway.

Standing almost seven-feet tall, were two large statues carved out of black stone; they had the bodies of human men but the faces of dogs. The heads were <u>adorned</u> with royal coverings and their waists were draped in fabric. Each statue held a massive weapon made from solid gold; their weapons crisscrossing one another.

CRASH!

A chest of scrolls collided with the ground, sending handwritten scrolls all over the place. Miguel's face was filled with guilt as he looked from the scrolls to Niyah then back to the scrolls then to Hugo.

"Uhhhhh, I thought I saw some clothes in that pile of loot," Miguel admitted, rubbing his hand on the back of his neck. "Something to help us *blend in*; you guys don't think we can just *walk* around Egypt with what we have on do you?" he finished.

"Good point, they'd probably think we were from another *galaxy*! Come on Hugo, we need to find some fabric to wrap over our clothes." Niyah answered, finally rolling the map clenched in her hand and placing it in her backpack.

One mile up the road from the <u>Valley of the Kings</u>, Prince Tutankhamun accompanied his friend Prince Amir of the <u>Kushite Kingdom</u> by royal chariot. Inside the carriage, the two princes examined a precious gift the Pharaoh sent back with Prince Amir; a telescope made of complete gold.

"Amir, you are looking through the wrong end my friend. Here…try this," instructed Prince Tut, as Prince Amir finally peered through the eye piece correctly over the vast land of Egypt.

The horses neighed loudly as the chariot came to a gradual stop alongside the west bank of the Nile River. Several steps away, a Kushite chariot waited for its Prince to return.

The Egyptian imperial guard steering the chariot stepped down from his seat and opened the door for the young princes to step down.

"Tut, this is incredible! My clan is most grateful for this gift from the Pharaoh!" replied Prince Amir, as he and the Prince jumped from the chariot, completely bypassing the step stool the royal guard was holding in place.

"Your happiness fills me with joy brother; I hope our fathers can come to a peace agreement soon. Our people should not be at war with one another," said Prince Tut, as he rotated the layers

of telescope to focus on the pyramids in the valley up ahead. *"Have a safe journey back home,"* he finished, handing Amir the golden telescope. The princes walked to the Kushite chariot and bid farewell to one another; Prince Tutankhamun stared in the distance at the Valley of the Kings as he slowly walked back.

"Boaz, I think I'll take a quick walk through the Imperial Valley" Tut said to his royal guard.

"Whatever you wish my lord, I will accompany you at once," replied Boaz, grabbing his sword from the chariot seat and strapping it onto his waist.

"You are my most trusted guard Boaz but I think I will be safe on my own for a few minutes; seeing as this Valley is occupied by souls already in the next life," replied Tut, as he turned to walk downhill.

"Very well Prince, I will wait for you here," replied Boaz, clenching his sword with concern.

After opening the tenth chest of gems and gold coins, Niyah, Hugo, and Miguel *finally* discovered one filled with the finest fabrics. Niyah managed to drape the Egyptian cotton and silk into a long dress while also concealing her backpack; the twins looked as if they were wearing togas but with some rope around their waists to serve as belts.

"We look pretty convincing," said Miguel, *completely* impressed with his draping skills.

"Yeah, we're not too shabby," agreed Niyah smiling.

"Sooo, where's the exit?" asked Hugo turning in circles as if there would be a neon-red *EXIT* sign blinking somewhere overhead.

"Right...*there,*" answered Niyah, walking back towards the sacred statues curiously.

"I read in a book once that Ancient Egyptians would set traps *and* secret passageways in their pyramids. The traps would be for thieves and the passageways for family members who required access. Statues like *these* were able to open hidden doors when you activated the trigger..." she said, slowly uncrossing the statues' swords.

"Look!" shouted Hugo, pointing to the wall to the right of the statues.

Niyah jerked her shoulders up in fear of flying daggers or the floor falling from underneath them. Instead, the wall began to sink back and a portion of the stones shifted to the side; creating a doorway.

"Alright! Nice going Niyah!" said Miguel.

"Thanks..." she replied, taking a deep breath, "... come on, let's get out of here," and they rushed through the doorway.

Click!

Niyah froze, recognizing the strange clicking noise when

she stepped on a loose stone nestled in the floor; immediately alerting the tomb of intruders.

WHOOSH! WHOOSH!

A *massive* crescent blade swung down from the ceiling, rocking from left to right, *directly* across the passageway and into slits on both sides of the walls.

"Are - you - KIDDING ME?" shouted Niyah, almost dropping the torch clenched in her hand.

WHOOSH! WHOOSH!

"We have to get by *that* thing?" Hugo asked, as he bit his lip.

"*Yeahhh*…we may want to just get back to the clubhouse," said Miguel, his eyes moving with the motion of the pendulum.

WHOOSH! WHOOSH!

"Ok, ok, ok…I need to think…there has to be a way around this trap. We can do this, <u>twaweza</u>, we can do this," Niyah chanted out loud; flowing between English and Swahili into a trance.

WHOOSH! WHOOSH!

"Niyah! It's O-K!" Hugo shouted, "We can just tell Mrs. Ridley that we had to choose between finding Tut and our own *lives!*"

"We can do this, twaweza, twaweza, twaweza..." she continued, shoving the torch into Hugo's hand without even looking at him; instead, her *eyes* were focused on the swinging blade.

WHOOSH! WHOOSH!

"I'm sure Mrs. Ridley will understand Niyah! ARE YOU EVEN LISTENING TO US?" Miguel demanded, shaking Niyah out of her bi-lingual daze.

"Nope," she admitted, "But I *have* figured out how to get past the blade, which *just* so happens to be swinging in *perfect* sequence."

"Why didn't you say so!" the twins answered.

WHOOSH! WHOOSH!

"The blade swings across every seven seconds; that means as long as we stay close to the wall-"

"We can slide past," Hugo interrupted.

"*Exactly*," Niyah answered, smiling proudly.

WHOOSH! WHOOSH!

"I'll go first," answered Hugo.

"No, *I'll* go first - I'm the oldest anyways," Miguel said as he past Hugo, snatched the torch, and stood in front of the swinging blade.

"There he goes again! Complete *lies!*" Hugo said laughing.

"*One, two, three four, five, six, seven-*" Miguel counted in his head before he moved another step; he decided to stay close to the left wall.

WHOOSH!

"*One, two, three, four, five, six, seven...*"

WHOOSH!

Miguel ran under the blade as quick as lightening, just as it reached the other side of the wall; exhaling only after he made it safely to the other side.

"Alright Miguel!"

"That's what I'm talking about!"

Niyah and Hugo cheered from the other side.

"Thank you, *thank you very much,*" Miguel answered in a voice like his homeroom teacher as he twisted a pretend mustache with his free hand, "Now it's time for you guys!"

"Ok, I'll go next but in case I don't make it, I just have to know..." Niyah said with a saddened look on her face.

WHOOSH! WHOOSH!

"…you guys don't actually like the cafeteria's *vomit-*flavored pasta salad right?" Niyah finished laughing.

"Don't make me puke Niyah!" Hugo said laughing. "Now focus on the death-blade in front of you please."

WHOOSH! WHOOSH!

One by one, Niyah and Hugo took their time counting the seconds in between the blade swinging across the hall and sprinted to safety.

"Now, let's get *out* of here," said Niyah as they walked further into the corridor towards a light in the distance.

"Doesn't it feel like we're walking up to the surface?" asked Hugo, as they finally reached the bright light flooding through a large square hole in a wooden door.

"I guess we don't need this torch anymore," said Miguel, waving it frantically until the fire went out.

They all pushed their weight against the door, scrapping the floor with their feet.

SLAM!

The door fell over and they were out of the royal hollows and one step closer to finding Tut.

"Finally! *Freedom!*" yelled Hugo, throwing himself to the desert sands. "OW!" he yelped, jumping back up to his feet, "This sand is HOT!"

They adjusted their disguises before walking uphill away from what they now realized was a valley filled with tombs and chambers carved into shallow stone peaks. Niyah pulled out her compass holding it steady until she <u>triangulated</u> north.

"Ok, guys…according to my compass, north is *this* direction. We can use the Nile River as a guide and follow it until we…*ummm…*" Niyah drifted off trying to find the right words to finish her instructions.

"*Bump* into Tut?" finished Miguel.

"Time for some <u>improv</u>," said Niyah, shrugging her shoulders.

"Good thing we're experts at that," remarked Miguel.

"Yup! We sure are," agreed Niyah.

"Come on then!" said Hugo, as he continued walking.

The dessert sun blazed upon the *already* hot sand as they made their way upwards out of the valley. Their invisible path winded and turned around many hills as Niyah, Miguel, and Hugo hiked through the fiery sands. Vultures circled high above, watching their three potential targets *very* carefully. The twins had their arms across each other's shoulders; *both* complaining that the *other* was dragging his feet.

"What's in your shoes bro? Bricks?" howled Miguel.

"What's in yours, cement blocks?" answered Hugo.

Niyah laughed and kept her eye on her compass as they walked over one steep hill after another out of the valley and towards the Nile River. The sweat was dripping down her face, stinging her eyes when she blinked. Suddenly, a small glimmer of light caught her attention from the corner of her eye.

"Hey, get down!" whispered Niyah.

The Gonzales brothers quickly responded, toppling over Niyah in the process; exhaustion must have taken over their precision.

"Ow!" howled Niyah, louder than she intended to.

"What is it?" whispered Hugo, rolling off of Niyah's arm.

"Down that hill, over there on the right, something bright was flashing…*Miguel, you're crushing my leg!*"

"Oh, sorry!" replied Miguel, moving his knee off of the back of her calf.

They slowly raised their heads over the hiding spot and were completely surprised to find a boy walking around aimlessly at the entrance of a tomb. He wore clothes similar to theirs but seemed to have on some sort of golden helmet, which reflected the sun's rays far into the distance.

"The flashing is coming from that kid," whispered Hugo, lifting his head obviously high over the mound; only to find that *kid* looking *back* at him.

"Keep your head down," sniped Miguel, pulling Hugo down by the hem of his clothes.

"Listen guys, we need to come up with a plan," said Niyah studying her compass. "We need to reach the palace without being detected and right about now, we're *roasting* in a desert valley…" she finished, wiping her forehead with the strap of her gown.

"How about we wait until tonight to travel?" asked Miguel.

"*Uh uh*! Not *me*! Who knows *what* comes out at night in Egypt! There could be snake-s! There could be scorpion-s! There could be…lion-s-s-s, with an *'s'*" replied Hugo.

"You have a good point Hugo," said Niyah smirking, "It's safer to travel during the day. Now that we've answered *that* question - we need to find another way to travel *besides* our shaky legs. No telling *how* long it'll take to reach the royal grounds let alone *find* Tut!"

"Speaking of Tut, how *are* we going to track him down exactly?" Miguel asked, taking off one of his sneakers to shake some sand out.

"Looking for the royal Prince, are you?" asked a foreign voice.

They cautiously turned around and to their surprise, the mystery kid, who was snooping around the valley just a moment ago, was now standing right in front of them.

"He looks like a god," thought Niyah, her jaw dropping in wonder.

He was completely covered in gold, from the bracelets and rings on his wrists and fingers to the golden ring around his bicep; even his sandals looked as though they were woven with rope dipped in gold. There was golden dust traced around his eyes and he wore a golden crown with a cobra snake sculpted in the front; the crown being the strange object they noticed glistening in the desert heat. All of this gold shined on his dark skin; making him appear as if he was glowing *himself.*

"Yeah, know where we can find him?" Miguel spoke up, as he put his sneaker back on.

"That would depend, what is the reason you seek the Prince?" the boy asked, looking from Miguel, to Hugo, to Niyah.

"We just want to…to… talk to him; *yeah* that's it," Hugo added, convincing himself of his own answer.

"No one is allowed to speak with Prince Tutankhamen unless they are a part of the royal assembly; *no one*. He does not even have someone to call 'friend' and often spends his time watching the children of the land playing together using his telescope," he replied, looking slightly upset.

Niyah looked at the twins with a puzzled look, *"How does he know such personal details about the Prince?"* she thought.

"So, can you hook us up?" asked Miguel.

"You foreigners speak amusingly, what object do you wish to '*hook*?'" the boy asked as he began to laugh; quickly erasing the worried look he had a moment earlier.

"*That's it, he knows how to get to the Prince and I'm going to MAKE him tell me,*" Niyah thought as she rose to her feet and took a step up onto the peak of the hill; she was standing eye to eye with him.

"Not *only* are we foreigners," Niyah said taking a step towards him, "We're from the *future,* sent here to help the Prince at the most crucial point in his *life*!"

He took a step back; maybe in caution or maybe in amazement of Niyah's secret <u>revelation</u>.

"We had to *bust* out of a tomb, risk getting our heads *chopped* off from a booby-trap *swinging* from the *ceiling*, climb over *hill* after *hill* in this *never-ending* valley, *just* to discover the location of the Nile so we can follow it to the Palace," Niyah continued, now panting from a combination of the extreme heat and her long speech.

"So, I only have *one* question for you, *golden boy*, can you take us to Prince Tut or *not?*"

Slowly, the mystery kid started smiling, taking a step closer to Niyah. In fact, he was admiring her soft features as the light wind blew Niyah's curls into the air and out of her face. Hugo and Miguel jumped to her defense, standing on either side of Niyah ready to strike. He looked at their faces and their shabby clothing as he thought about the incredible information just shared.

"You speak the truth…for that reason, I will help you," he responded.

"*I* am Prince Tutankhamen."

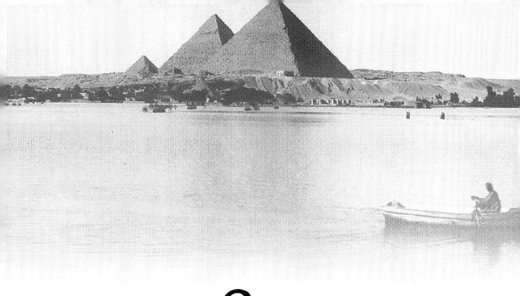

8

RACE AGAINST THE NILE

"WHAAAT?" screeched Hugo, quickly clasping his hands over his mouth.

"*Alright*, we found him!" Miguel said, grabbing a hold of Niyah and Hugo around their shoulders in celebration but Niyah's cheeks became rosy pink from embarrassment; she was worried she insulted Tut.

"Prince-I-uh…" she attempted to explain but fumbled over her words.

"It is quite alright, you have a *very* firm hand when

needed, that will be useful for you in life," Tut <u>interjected</u>.

"Thank you…I guess proper introductions are in order. My name is Niyah Zuri and these *bodyguards* are the Gonzales twins, Hugo and Miguel," she replied.

"It is truly an honor to meet you all," said Tut. "Please, follow me to my chariot; I am eager to hear *all* about the future!" he said, pointing to a horse-pulled carriage in the distance.

"Thanks man, I need to get out of this *heat*!" Hugo replied, wiping away the sticky sweat now trickling down his face.

As they walked away from the Valley of the Kings, Tut pointed in various directions while explaining the rich history of Egypt, the wars with the <u>Hittites</u> of the North, the current peace talks with the <u>Kushites</u> of the South, and the beautiful northern Palace his father completed a few years before he was born.

"My Prince…" bowed the royal guard as the group finally reached the chariot, "…it seems that you have collected some friends while you were away."

"Greetings Boaz…yes, I have made some friends during my walk. This is Niyah…from the Kingdom of Kush and her…skilled guards from <u>Arabia</u>." Tut introduced convincingly.

"Greetings"

"*Cool* sword man"

"Wasss-uppppp," they all greeted, following Tut into the shaded chariot.

"*What did those Arabians say?*" thought Boaz, as he mounted his seat to steer the royal chariot back to the Palace.

The interior of the chariot was upholstered with a deep purple velvet, there were two long seats on both sides, and the ceiling was embroidered magnificently with the image of a sun rising over a pyramid. Tut and Hugo sat on one side while Niyah and Miguel sat on the other, listening closely to Tut's history lesson.

"…and over there is the town of Luxor and this glorious river is the Nile, which our scholars believe is the longest river in Alkebulan!" said Tut.

"WOW! Alkebulan really *is* the original name for Africa!" Niyah interrupted excitedly. "The Greeks eventually called it Ethiopia then a bunch of other names came and went, until the Romans gave it the final name; *Africa.* That's what we call this land in the future - and about the Nile, it's actually the longest river in the *world…oh…whoops…*I was going all bookworm again wasn't I?" asked Niyah.

"*Yup!*" said the twins laughing; Niyah tucked her lips into her mouth for safe keeping.

"How big *is* the world exactly," Tut asked, his eye wide with curiosity.

"*Well*, you already know how big Africa is, so imagine seven more land masses the same size," began Miguel… ."*Then*, throw in some large bodies of water separating *all* that land, like oceans, seas, and *so* many rivers, lakes, ponds, streams, creeks…*man*, I'm starting to sound like Niyah!" finished Hugo as they all laughed.

"So, what do you do for fun around here?" asked Niyah, releasing herself from verbal prison.

"We do many things! There's Senet, which my father is still instructing me through, more of a <u>strategic</u> game with individual pieces you move on a board. I look forward to showing you, perhaps before our evening meal? There are the yearly harvest games, where players compete in different rounds of challenges that display their strength and skill and of course there's Crocodile Nile; a game I *personally* created," replied Tut with a huge grin on his face.

"*Crocodile* Nile? Wi- wi-with *actual* crocodiles?" asked Hugo, pointing out of the window towards the river.

"That is correct…would you like to play?" asked Tut.

They realized then and there that Tut also had a love for adventure. Without waiting for a reply, he promptly signaled Boaz to halt the chariot.

"So, the race begins with two small reed boats, which I *just* so happen to have on board in case my friend Prince Amir wished to play during our long journey; he and I have become quite the experts," said Tut as he leaped from the carriage.

"But there's four of us Tut, are we playing doubles?" Niyah asked, already tying her hair back into a ponytail.

"That is correct," he answered, now noticing Hugo was the only one still sitting in the chariot.

"Hugo my friend, you shall be my partner. I have won this race *many* times, you have nothing to fear!" Tut said.

"I've heard *that* before, 'nothing to fear but fear itself', right?" asked Hugo, as he dragged himself from the chariot as *slow* as *humanly* possible.

"The goal of the game is to navigate your boat through the many obstacles found in the Nile, such as hippos and *specifically* the crocodiles," Tut instructed.

"Nice of you to mention the Hippos Tut," said Miguel laughing. "Not like *they* could eat us or anything."

"Do not worry my friends, hippos represent the <u>goddess Tauret</u> and crocodiles the <u>god Sobek.</u> As these gods protect my people, so do the creatures in this very river; we will be safe. Now let us continue!" shouted Tut.

"So, the first boat to reach the end is the winner?" asked Hugo, testing his paddling-style in the air with both hands (he was determined to at least warm-up before being eaten alive).

"Yes, correct again" answered Tut, now dragging one boat toward the river's edge.

"The end of *where* exactly?" asked Niyah, now bringing the other reed boat close by her.

"Boaz will ride ahead of us, stopping several miles outside of the royal grounds. Once our race is complete, we can relax in my carriage, giving us a chance to rest before you all meet the Pharaoh and Queen Nefertiti," explained Tut, holding on to his boat as the river's strength attempted to pull it away.

"*We* get to meet *them*? Niyah asked, blinking in disbelief.

"Of course! Now let us begin!" replied Tut, signaling Hugo to join him in the boat.

Niyah quickly unveiled her compass to check their coordinates before placing it securely in her backpack and fastening the straps. With Hugo finally on board (both emotionally and physically), Miguel and Niyah entered their boat and were ready to take off as Tut did a countdown.

"Three! Two! One!"

Miguel used his paddle to push their boat far from the edge and Niyah began paddling on the left side as Miguel steered the boat with his paddle from the back.

"LET'S GET THESE GUYS!" Niyah shouted, paddling with all her strength.

"I'M RIGHT BEHIND YOU…LITERALLY!" answered Miguel, now paddling to steer the boat around Tut and Hugo.

"HUGO! PADDLE RIGHT! PADDLE RIGHT! WE NEED TO STOP THEM!" shouted Tut up ahead.

"AY-YIY TUT!" Hugo yelled, suddenly steering the boat at a sharp angle; in less than 10 seconds it would crash directly into the other.

"MIGUEL, WATCH OUT! HUGO'S GONNA SMASH INTO US!" Niyah warned, now using her paddle to slow down the boat. Miguel instantly following her <u>tactic</u>.

Their boat halted *just* in time; Tut nearly fell into the Nile as his boat hit the river's edge, sending a strong vibration in the current.

BOOM!

"Careful Hugo! You do not want to be the one responsible for drowning the Prince!" Tut said, laughing.

Slowly, its flat head rose to the surface, followed by three more; their copper-colored eyes glaring at the boats floating towards them.

"Maybe we should switch places, you can steer in the back and I'll guide in the front?" suggested Hugo, holding tightly to the side of the boat as they switched.

"That is a great idea," answered Tut.

"Well, I'm known to have *many* of those," Hugo said boastfully, as Tut took his seat. "YOU GUYS ALRIGHT?" Hugo shouted, signaling to Niyah and Miguel with both arms above his head; their faces were filled with panic.

"Miguel, Niyah, good strategy! Ready to begin once more?" Tut yelled back but realized they were focused on something more interesting up ahead.

"Hell-oooo?" Hugo yelled, waving his arms back and forth, "EARTH TO NIYAH! MIGUEL, WHATS UP WITH YOU BRO?"

As Tut turned around to face forward, he saw them; all *eight* of them.

"Hugo, time to get going," Tut whispered, slowly grabbing his paddle.

"LET'S GET OUT OF HERE!" Niyah finally shouted as she and Miguel sent their paddles thrashing in the water.

Hugo whipped his head around, now staring at what everyone else had already seen up ahead; *crocodiles*.

They all paddled their way up the river, carefully avoiding the terrifying crocs. They had already passed three of the ancient creatures when Tut felt his paddle being pulled into the water; by the *largest* crocodile of the group.

"He's destroying my paddle Hugo!" Tut shouted, eventually letting go of his paddle and watching it sink to the bottom.

"What are we going to do?" Hugo yelled, alternating his paddling to both sides of the boat.

"Niyah, we have to help them!" Miguel screamed and they both started paddling harder until they're boats lined up.

"Quick, get in!" Niyah shouted, as she held both boats together with her paddle. Hugo and Tut quickly jumped into the other boat with their *one* surviving paddle.

"What are those children up to?" Boaz thought, trying to decipher what was happening in the distance.

"Thank you, friends, but we must get out of this river *at once!*" Tut commanded.

"Fine by me!" the twins yelled.

"Look! Up ahead, the right side of the river bank is clear. We should be able to make it there before the crocs catch up!" Niyah instructed. "Come on, let's go!"

Using the remaining three paddles, they steered the boat rapidly, curving around the remaining seven crocodiles with ease.

"Why aren't they chasing us Tut?" Miguel asked, rowing

in the back of the boat.

"They are territorial beings, only attacking if threatened. I must have hit one with my paddle by accident," Tut said.

"Yeah and he had your paddle as a woody snack!" Miguel said.

"Look guys! We're almost at the river bank!" Hugo shouted, handing his paddle to Tut to alternate rowing shifts.

"Just a bit further!" Niyah said, not realizing how deep she was thrusting the paddle into the water; until she *felt* it.

Thump!

Within two seconds a baby crocodile came leaping out of the water, mouth stretched wide, and teeth thrashing. Its copper eyes squinted as its jaw closed down on Niyah's paddle; whipping its long spiky tail into the water.

SPLASH!

"WATCH OUT!" Tut shouted as Niyah tried to rip her paddle out of the baby crocodile's sharp clenches.

SPLASH!

"MY PRINCE!" Boaz shouted, leaping from the chariot seat and plunging straight into the river.

"JUST LET IT GO, NIYAH!" Hugo shouted, holding on to her shoulders so she wouldn't be pulled overboard.

"IF I LET GO, WE WON'T MAKE IT TO THE RIVERBANK! WE ONLY HAVE THREE PADDLES LEFT" Niyah screamed, pulling again on her paddle lodged in the croc's mouth. Suddenly, the baby crocodile's mother decided to join the party, appearing from the river below.

SPLASH!

"NIYAH! LET-IT-GO!" Miguel demanded, now paddling on one side of boat, sending all of them in a dizzying circle. Niyah slipped back, crushing Hugo's arm but managed to free her paddle.

Boaz was swimming at maximum speed, lifting his head out of the water every five seconds to shout, "MY LORD!"

"I am beginning to feel unwell" Tut slurred and quickly clasped two hands over his mouth.

Maybe it was the nausea or the fact that their heads felt woozy but all of a sudden everything felt like it was happening in *slow motion*:

Miguel – stops paddling

Two large nostrils - come rising up from the water

Niyah – jaw drops

Hugo – eyes bulge out

Nostrils – belong to a large headed creature

Tut – drops hands, starts grinning

Hippo's massive body – smashes into the large croc

Croc is dragged – into the abyss

Bubbles rise to the surface – from the depths of the River Nile

"Did you see that?" Miguel asked, shaking his head in disbelief.

"I certainly did!" Tut answered and he began to paddle once more.

"That-was-AWESEOME!" Hugo shouted, rubbing his achy shoulder; the one that Niyah *crushed* with her *entire* body.

"Was that a *Hippo*?" Niyah asked, blinking in amazement as she started to row with whatever was *left* of her paddle.

They reached the edge of the river bank just as Boaz was pulling himself out of the water.

"Boaz!" Tut yelled as they jumped out of the boat; completely forgetting to pull it out.

"My Prince! Lord Tut! I hope no harm has come to you!" a drenched Boaz shouted, as he pounded his right fist across his heart and kneeled.

Squish!

"Thank you, Boaz, we are all fine! The mighty goddess Tauret kept us all safe!" Tut exclaimed, as he hugged his new friends.

Squish!

"Crocodile Nile sure lived up to its name...and the *teeth* on that baby croc! I was impressed!" Niyah said, smiling with relief.

"They are truly amazing creatures. How about we continue on to the palace?" Tut suggested, as he walked over to the chariot's storage compartment to put away the remaining paddles. Niyah finished squeezing her damp curls and followed Tut to store her trophy paddle.

"Sounds good to me!" said Miguel, wringing the water from his drenched clothing with both hands.

"Yeah, I could use some food!" Hugo added, shaking his head sideways to drain the water lodged in his ears.

"Then to the palace we go! Boaz, thank you my faithful guardian, I do not need to fear with you in my presence." Tut stated, now pounding his right fist across his heart and nodding his head.

"It is my *honor* Prince Tutankhamen," Boaz answered rising; leaving a small pool of water at his feet.

They all jumped into the chariot's plush interior, completely exhausted from their race against the famous

Nile River. Within minutes of their journey, Tut continued to narrate Egyptian history with <u>extravagant</u> detail. Niyah laid her head back to stare at the gold embroidered ceiling; imagining Tut's words in her mind...

Pharaohs...

The royal family...

<u>*Legacies...*</u>

9

THE SENET CHALLENGE

"Watson! Look what I've found!" Niyah shouted, as she brushed away more dirt from the ancient bones.

"Dr. Zuri! This is remarkable! You have done it!" Watson exclaimed as he took out a camera to begin documenting the discovery.

"After all these years! I've finally found her! The <u>Mayan</u> Priestess I learned of when I was only a child!" Niyah exclaimed. She carefully removed some dirt from an <u>ornate</u> jade necklace, which managed to never leave its ancient owner's throat.

"Paging Dr. Zuri!" shouted Watson; Niyah looked up in confusion.

"Watson, what are you talking about, I'm right here," she replied, shaking her head.

"Doctor Zuuurrriiii!" he continued...

"Come in Niyah!"

"Earth to Niyah!"

Niyah's eye sprang open, glancing out of the carriage at the violet and pink hues painted across the sky.

"It's about time sleeping beauty," said Miguel chuckling.

"I had the weirdest dream," Niyah replied, now sitting up in her seat.

"Yeah, we know!" said Hugo, "Who's Watson?"

"No *clue!*" she said laughing.

"Welcome back Niyah," Tut greeted, "We are approaching the Palace, are you all hungry?"

"You could say that again!" the twins replied.

"As you wish…are you all hungry?" Tut repeated, causing the Gonzales twins to burst out laughing.

"No Tut, it's just an expression…" Miguel replied,

holding his stomach as he tried to stop laughing.

"It means 'yes'," Hugo explained, taking a deep breathe to calm down.

Gurrrgle

Niyah's stomach grumbled answering Tut before she even had a chance.

"I think it's from all the rowing…" she explained, smiling at the memory of the Nile, "…or the crocodile evading, one or the other."

"Then I am glad our journey is complete; may I welcome you all to the Northern Palace of Pharaoh Akhenaten," Tut said, pointing out across the royal land to the glowing palace they were quickly approaching. The palace towered high above the ground, with a grand staircase leading to the main entranceway. There were large fire pits on either side of the main gate and countless soldiers protecting *every* square inch of the area. When the carriage finally halted, the scent of exotic oils and incense burning in the air <u>engulfed</u> them; it smelled like Egypt.

"Tut, it's beautiful!" Niyah said. The Prince watched as Niyah smiled at the stunning surroundings.

"I am glad it pleases you, come, let us all go inside. I want you to meet my parents!" Tut replied as he leaped from the chariot, completely bypassing the step stool.

The three of them followed Tut into the palace, passing many dark lit rooms glowing with candlelight until they finally reached Tut's quarters.

"Your Highness, welcome!" greeted the guard posted at the entrance of Tut's chambers.

"Good evening Kizza, I have brought friends with me to attend this evening's meal," Tut replied, as his guard opened the wooden double doors to his room (Kizza watched the foreign guests with much suspicion).

Niyah's eyes widened as she scanned the room in amazement; it was the size of her *classroom*. There was a large bed on the right side of the room with a nearby desk containing jars filled with numerous scrolls. All of the walls were decorated with Egyptian paintings, separated by hanging spears, arrows, and other weapons. Another area to the left was for lounging; there were enormous floor pillows hand stitched with the same golden-sun design found inside Tut's personal chariot. Next to the floor pillows was a small table with two chairs on either side; something that looked like a chessboard was set on top.

"Cool room, Tut," Miguel said, as he stretched across a floor pillow, arms crossed behind his head.

"Yeah, *really* cool," said Hugo, inspecting the weaponry on one of the walls with deep curiosity. "Do you ever get to *use* these things?" he asked, pointing to a large ax-like weapon.

 |94   *NIYAH ZURI & THE PHARAOH'S THRONE*

"No Hugo, they are for honoring my ancestors; my father's father and his father and even his father before him, used these weapons to protect our land... but *sometimes,*" Tut continued in a half whisper, "Boaz will take one down for me to spar with."

"*Niiice,*" Hugo answered with a grin, as he walked over to plop on a nearby pillow; causing Miguel to roll out of his relaxed pose and onto his face.

"Tut, what's this game?" Niyah asked pointing to the table, completely ignoring Miguel whopping his brother's head between two enormous pillows; his version of sweet revenge.

"*This* Niyah, is Senet; less of a game and *more* of a journey. My father says I will be ready for the throne when I am able to gain victory over him in Senet but he is a masterful player," explained Tut, as he stared at the game board.

"Cut yourself some slack Tut, you're only eight," said Miguel, releasing Hugo from his pillow attacks.

"I will be nine by the next full moon. At my age, my father was already able to master this game and my grandfather allowed him to sit in with the counsel," replied Tut.

"Maybe we can help! What are the rules for Senet?" asked Niyah, as she placed her backpack on the right arm of the challenger's seat and sat down; Tut's face shined with hope.

"Listen *carefully*: The board has thirty squares, comprised of three rows of ten. We each have our own set of pawns and the goal is to make it to your opponent's side of the board. Now, you must be careful…" Tut explained, as five minutes turned into 10 and then in 30 until he fully clarified the rules.

"Understand?" Tut eventually asked.

"Got it" answered Niyah, realizing just then that the twins had fallen asleep on the royal pillows.

"WAKE UP GONZALES BOYS!" Niyah shouted, interrupting the twins' harmonious snoring. Even in sleep, Hugo and Miguel were in perfect unison.

"Hu? What? Senet? Who won?" asked Miguel, wiping his drool with his shirt.

"Tut just finished explaining the rules, now it's time for the challenge," Niyah answered.

The twins stood up and walked over to the board game, standing on either side of Tut and Niyah. Tut's smile slowly faded into a stern line as he stated, "Your move." Niyah's face did the same.

They played Senet until the sun began to set over the horizon; each attempting to predict the other's strategy.

"Nice move Niyah," Hugo praised, then Tut moved his next piece; swiftly collecting Niyah's pawn as another prize.

"Boo-yah! In your FACE!" Miguel shouted; he could feel Niyah's eye's glaring into the side of his head.

Suddenly, Kizza rushed through the doors into Tut's quarters.

"Prince, I have urgent news! Your father has fallen ill and is requesting your presence!" he shouted.

"I will join him at once!" Tut replied and quickly ran out into the hall.

"This is the moment isn't it?" Hugo asked, looking at the unfinished Senet game.

Tut quickly climbed many steps, passing endless walls of artwork that depicted his royal lineage. He ran *so* fast, the images were beginning to spin around in his head until he finally reached the doors of the King's chambers. The guards stepped aside and the Prince slowly pushed the tall doors open.

Back in Tut's room, Niyah was lost in a daze. She stared out into the distance at the pyramids, royal quarters, temples, and dwellings. The sweet and spicy scent of incense was carried in the wind as she looked outward towards the nearby horse's stables. Time felt still, as if the earth itself slowed to a quiet halt. The eerie silence finally broke by the shrill of cries echoing from the quarters above…

"Yeah, this is it," answered Niyah.

"I thought we time travelled to *help* Tut not be a part of his *misery*," Miguel <u>lamented</u>, as he walked across the room in the same footpath.

"Mrs. Ridley's instructions said we need to help him *'during the most critical point in his life'* but how?" Niyah added.

"Maybe we help him write his speech - like when the President wins an election," Hugo suggested, as he tried to pull an arrowhead off the wall of weapons.

"Or maybe he needs our help to set some new laws around here," said Miguel, now sitting at the Senet table staring at Hugo's <u>feeble</u> attempts to remove the arrowhead.

The hours were blending together; no one had a *clue* what time it was. Niyah buried herself underneath a pile of floor pillows while the twins tried the strength of two on the wall of weapons.

"Some kind of mission this was," thought Niyah, as she breathed in the fine Egyptian silk. *"We came all this way…there must be something we can do to help Tut…"* she thought, sighing in the stillness of her pillow cocoon.

Slowly, the main doors to the chambers creaked open and in he walked…the *new* Pharaoh.

The twins silently watched Tut as he locked his door, crossed the room, and sat quietly on the edge of his bed.

"Umm…Niyah?" Hugo whispered; those two simple words unleashed Niyah from her pyramid of pillows.

"*Tut!*" she thought rising quickly, sending pillows flying all around her.

"Hi Tut…" Niyah said softly, choosing her words carefully; cautiously approaching him as if he were a raging lion in the African bush. His eyes were puffy and his face was completely blank of expression.

"We know what happened…there's no need to explain…" she continued, Tut was absolutely still.

"We're here to help you bro!" Miguel blurted out, startling the young Prince from his deepest thoughts.

"Help? HELP!" Tut finally answered, his eyes narrowed and full of anger.

Niyah took a few steps back from the furious lion.

"How can I be King of Egypt? I could not even master Senet!" he shouted, leaping from his bed to his window, searching for the words to express his pain…and fear.

"This *land*… all of these *people*…are now *my* responsibility!" Tut shouted, looking out at the horizon as the sun's rays began to rise.

"Listen Tut, you can *do* this," Miguel said, slowly walking over to the window.

"Yeah bro, you're a Prince - you've probably been waiting for this day your whole life," Hugo added, finally giving up on the arrowhead to join his brother's side.

"That's it!" thought Niyah, rushing to her backpack and quickly unzipping it to find the one piece of proof Tut may believe.

"It is true, I have studied to lead my people but I did not think…that my *father*…not like *this*…" Tut stammered, not taking his eyes off the rising sun.

"If you don't get it *together* Tutankhamen, you will be sacrificing *all* of *this*!" Niyah shouted, successfully breaking Tut's eye trance. Turning around, they saw Niyah kneeling on the floor pointing to what she unrolled; the map.

Curious, Tut walked closer and kneeled on the other side of the map for a closer look.

"This is a timeline of all the important travel points in the past, present, and future," Niyah explained, pointing to the scribbled writing. Tut examined the map, straining his eyes to read the various markers on the timeline.

Slowly, a new marker began to appear on the map, Egypt, 1337 B.C.

"If you didn't become a mighty Pharaoh, we wouldn't *be*

here. We were sent to help you and now I know for what…" she finished.

"You do?" the twins asked, walking over to join them.

"We're here to help you believe…believe in *yourself*" Niyah said, smiling with accomplishment.

"Tut, your people *need* you…not being able to master Senet shows that you still have more to learn and only the wisest of Pharaoh's could admit that," she finished, looking up to meet his golden eyes.

"Wisest of Pharaoh's…" Tut repeated, <u>contemplating</u> Niyah's words.

"*Wisest*," Niyah confirmed.

"You're gonna be a legend," Hugo said, taking a seat next to Tut.

"Like I already said, you can do this Tut," Miguel added, as he sat in between Hugo and Niyah.

"Thank you…friends," Tut replied, with hope finally filling his eyes.

"I'm sure your father will pass on his blessing…from the next life." Niyah said.

"The Queen is upstairs already making preparations…I just hope I can be a great leader like my father-" Tut began to reply but was suddenly cut off.

BANG-BANG-BANG!

"PRINCE!" Kizza shouted!

"Open this door at once! We think the Pharaoh may have been poisoned and your new friends are under suspicion!" Kizza yelled.

"Lies!" Tut yelled, "They have been alongside me all day; they did not do this Kizza!"

"UNLOCK THIS DOOR OR I WILL BREAK IT DOWN!" Kizza threatened; pounding harder and harder on the wooden entry.

BANG-BANG-BANG!

"Guys, we have to get out of here!" Niyah shouted, "Quick, we need to open the portal!"

"See ya Tut and good luck," Miguel said.

BANG-BANG-BANG!

"Thanks for the fun on the River, you'll make a cool Pharaoh," said Hugo, as he gave Tut his first-ever first-bump.

"Tut," Niyah said, hugging her new friend. As she pulled away, she looked into the Pharaoh's scared eyes and told him firmly, "Believe in yourself."

"TUTANKHAMEN! THIS IS YOUR LAST WARNING!" Kizza threatened.

BANG-BANG-BANG!

"Thank you Niyah and thank you Gonzalez brothers..." Tut answered, hoping his door would hold up a few more minutes.

"Here, take this," Tut said, *easily* removing a single arrowhead from the wall of weapons and quickly tossing it to Niyah.

Catching it firmly, Niyah smiled back at Tut but there was no time for any of that.

BANG-BANG-BANG!

"We need to get back to the clubhouse," Niyah said closing her eyes. She concentrated as hard as she could on getting back to Xavier before they were tossed in an Egyptian prison cell...or worse.

"Ready guys?"

"Ready!"

"TO SOLVE PAST MYSTERIES, TRUE SEEKERS OF KNOWLEDGE NEED YOU BE, THEN YOU CAN UNLOCK THE SECRETS OF HISTORY..."

SMASH!

Kizza along with three other *persistent* guards broke through the door.

"GRAB THEM!" Kizza commanded.

"NO!" Tut screamed, leaping in Kizza's path.

"...BUT YOU MUST USE THE POWER OF THREE!"

FLASH!

The spark of light consumed them instantly, sending Niyah, Hugo, and Miguel through a winding tunnel of darkness. The path of time and space created a <u>vortex</u> of feelings and memories that were replaying in Niyah's mind: escaping from the Valley of the tombs, finding Tut, almost being eaten by crocodiles, hanging out in the palace, learning to play Senet, Tut becoming Pharaoh overnight, those golden eyes of his...then just as quickly, they were back in the present.

Ooof!

Ugh!

Ow!

"*Aw man!* We really need to get better at this time traveling thing," Miguel said, lifting himself off the ground slowly.

"I second that bro," Hugo added, still lying on his side.

"There's always tomorrow," said Niyah, standing to brush the pine needles stuck to her Egyptian attire; the arrowhead never leaving her grasp.

"We actually did it; we helped Tut believe in himself!" Hugo said, straining to get up.

"Probably helped that he was all googley-eyed for Niyah," Miguel said laughing; Hugo didn't find it very funny.

"He was not Miguel…" Niyah said blushing, finally opening her hand to stare at the gift Tut gave her.

"And where have *you* three been?" questioned a high-pitched voice from behind.

The trespasser was standing with her arms crossed, tapping her foot impatiently, and completely decked out in head-to-toe pink-*overload*.

"*Oh no!*" Niyah thought, as she whipped her head around to face the intruder.

Mihn!

GLOSSARY

A

Accusations: charges of wrongdoing or fault

Adorned: decorated

Adrenaline: energy the brain creates to stimulate the body; normally created as a reaction to a situation, stress, or anger

Alkebulan: An ancient name of Africa that means 'Mother of Mankind'

Analyzing: to study

Ancient Egypt: An ancient civilization in Northeastern Africa along the Nile River; known for creating the first mathematical and astronomical systems

Andromeda: The Milky Way's neighbor galaxy; named after the Ethiopian Princess saved by Perseus in Greek mythology

Apache Warrior Geronimo: Apache Indian Chief who led battles to protect his tribe's land from the Mexican Army and

American Settlers in the late 1800s

Arabia: a peninsula in Southwest Asia, located to the east of Egypt, Africa

Atlantic Ocean: an ocean surrounded by North America and South America in the western hemisphere and Europe and Africa in the Eastern hemisphere; approximately 31.5 Million square miles

B

Boastfully: showing an extra amount of pride in one's achievements or abilities

C

Century: a period of 100 years

Chai tea: a mix of tea, herbs, and spices

Chao: Spanish for "bye"

Climate: an area's general weather

Colossal: extraordinarily great in size; gargantuan, gigantic

Contemplating: deeply thinking

Coordinates: a mathematical measurement of a location or point; latitude and longitude on a compass

Critical: of high importance

D

Decade: a time period of 10 years

Decipher: to interpret, translate, or discover

Distinguished: expressed dignity or high rank

Distributed: to divide or give out

Donde es mi: Spanish for "where is my"

E

Eerie: spooky, creepy, or strange

Empress: the female ruler of an empire (Emperor being the male ruler); higher rank than a king or queen; highest honor in a monarch.

Engulfed: surrounded

Extravagant: very fancy

F

Feeble: weak

Flora and fauna: plants and wildlife

G

Gargantuan: extraordinarily great in size; colossal, gigantic

God Sobek: Ancient Egyptian god depicted as a man with a crocodile head; offered protection against dangers in Nile River

Goddess Tauret: Ancient Egyptian goddess depicted as a pregnant woman with a Hippopotamus head, lion's legs, and crocodile's tail; helped the daily rebirth of the sun

H

Hieroglyphics: Ancient Egyptian writing comprised of symbols and pictures (similar to an alphabet)

Himalayas: a 1,500-mile mountain-range between Tibet and India

Hittites: an ancient people from Anatolia; modern-day Turkey Eastern Europe along the Mediterranean Sea; north of Egypt

Humidity: moist or damp air conditions

I

Improv: short for 'improvisation,' which means to perform or deliver without preparation

Incantation: the chanting of words with magical power

Interjected: interrupted

Intricate: complex or detailed

J

K

King Tutankhamen: the most well-known Ancient Egyptian Pharaoh who became King around 9 years old and ruled from 1332 BC-1323 BC

Kushite Kingdom: ancient African kingdom south of Egypt; modern-day Sudan; invaded and ruled Egypt in the 8th century; kingdom eventually conquered by the Kingdom of Axum

Kwaheri: Swahili for "goodbye"

L

Lamented: to express regret or disappointment

Legacies: history passed down from an ancestor or predecessor

M

Mali Empire: ancient West African empire that stretched from modern-day countries of Senegal to Niger; known for the great wealth of its rulers

Mars: fourth planet from the sun

Mayan: ancient civilization that encompassed modern-day

Southern Mexico and northern Central America; created written language of the Americas prior to Christopher Columbus

Michael Jordan: One of the greatest American Basketball players in history

Mt. Everest: the highest Mountain peak in the world; 29,028 feet high

N

Narrate: to tell a story of events

Nile River: the longest river in the world that originates from Lake Victoria in Uganda, Africa and flows north all the way through Egypt, Africa and into the Mediterranean Sea

O

Ornate: decorative or elaborate

P

Padparadscha: a rare sapphire with pink-orange hue; found in East Africa, Sri Lanka, and Vietnam

Parchment: a stiff material on which to write

Perro: Spanish for "dog"

Pharaoh: the title of an Ancient Egyptian King

Polaris: the name of the North Star

Portal: an entrance, gate, or door

Practical: straight-forward

Precision: accurate, true, or exact

President F.D.R.: Franklin Delano Roosevelt was the 32nd President of the U.S.A.; only President in US history to serve three terms (totaling 12 years)

Q

R

Revelation: something made known

S

Samurai: noble military warriors of Medieval and early-modern Japan; followed a set of rules known as Bushido or 'the way of the warrior'

Simultaneously: at the same time

Strategic: well thought-out

Supernova: the explosion of a star

T

Tactic: plan

Tanzania: a country in East Africa; rich in steel and iron; south of Uganda, Africa

Teleported: the act of teleportation; transporting a person or object by telekinesis across a distance instantaneously

The Milky Way: the galaxy in which the earth and the associated solar system belong; contains at least 100 billion stars

Tibet: a region in Asia north of the Himalayas once governed by the Dalai Lama for thousands of years as the Tibetan Empire, is a division of China today. As it relates to elevation; it is the highest region in the world for thousands of years as the Tibetan Empire, is a division of China today. As it relates to elevation; it is the highest region in the world

Triangulated: determining a location by measure angles from a known point to a fixed baseline; can be completed with a compass and/or a map

Triassic period: a geological period 230 – 190 million years ago when dinosaurs first roamed the earth; followed by the Jurassic and Cretaceous periods

Twaweza: Swahili for "we can do this"

U

Unforeseen: sudden or a surprise

Unison: together

V

Vague: not clear

Valley of the Kings: the royal tombs of Ancient Egyptian royalty located in a valley west of the Nile River in Egypt, Africa

Vortex: a whirling mass of water, air, or fire

W

Wilderness: a wild region; inhabited only by wild animals

X

Y

Yo no sé: Spanish for "I don't know"

Z

ABOUT THE AUTHOR

Anna Nyakana is an Award-Winning and Bestselling Author, Motivational Speaker, Entrepreneur, and Business Owner of Niyah Zuri Books and Niyah Zuri Studios. Anna was born in Berlin, Germany in 1986 to a Ugandan father and German-Moldavian mother. Her family immigrated to the United States in the early 90's, settling in Stamford, Connecticut. Anna pursued her writing and musical passions beginning at the age of 6 and spent her teenage years honing her skills of songwriting and live performance until releasing her debut album in 2007. Anna Nyakana proceeded to attain her Bachelor's degree in Business in 2011 and soon after extended her writing talents into her first literary work, "The *Student Survival Guide to Online College.*" She was able to guide thousands of students during their journey of attaining higher education through an online platform through this quick guide but yearned to help a different demographic close to her heart: children. Through her own personal experiences, Anna discovered there was an overwhelming need for multicultural children's books where heroines could slay the fiercest of dragons versus filling the typical princess in distress role. Out of this desire, the Niyah Zuri series was born and Anna took the next few years to write and publish her greatest literary work. *"Niyah Zuri and The Pharaoh's Throne"* hails as a time-bending exploration of ancient lands lead by the headstrong Niyah Zuri and her best friends Miguel and Hugo Gonzales. This chapter book is geared towards upper elementary through lower middle school readers and comes equipped with a full glossary and free online resources for parents and teachers to access.

Anna has been featured on many media outlets to spread the Niyah Zuri message including SiriusXM, Entercom Radio, NBC, ABC, FOX, and News 12 Connecticut. During her interview on SiriusXM's "The Karen Hunter Show," Anna stressed the importance of diversity in the classroom and the purpose of the Niyah Zuri series, "It *is critical children see a reflection of themselves in the books that they read. My mission is to inspire them, one adventure at a time.*" Working directly with school administrators in her state, she has implemented the Niyah Zuri series into the curriculum of several school districts and is working tirelessly to spread the Niyah Zuri message of representation, girl-empowerment, leadership, and world history across the country through in-school author visits and virtual lessons. *"Niyah Zuri and The Pharaoh's Throne"* and *"Niyah Zuri and The Mayan Eclipse"* are available on www.annanyakana.com, Amazon, Barnes & Noble, and all major bookstores and retailers. Anna Nyakana lives with her children in Connecticut, U.S.A.

What will happen...

...now that their secret is out?

The series continues in the next adventure of...

..."Niyah Zuri and The Mayan Eclipse"...

Made in the USA
Middletown, DE
13 November 2021